Surviving the BIKER

CASSIE ALEXANDRA

MORE BOOKS

Surviving the

BIKER

ONE

ADRIANA

"ADRIANA," SAID VANDA from the other side of the bathroom door. "Are you okay?"

I wiped my mouth with a tissue. "Yes," I replied, dropping it into the toilet. "I'll be out in a minute."

She was silent for a couple of seconds. "Are you throwing up again?"

"No," I lied. "I just finished brushing my teeth. What do you need, Mom?"

"I thought I heard you getting sick again. I'm just worried about you."

I turned on the water and began washing my hands, not sure whether to be angry or amused that she'd been listening outside of the door. "I'm fine. I'll be right out."

"Okay."

When I stepped out of the bathroom, she was still in my room, staring out of the window, a pensive look on her face.

"What's up?" I asked.

She turned and I could see that the worry lines on her face were deeper than usual. "I was going to ask you the same thing."

"I don't know what you mean," I said, walking over to my closet. I slid the door open and began looking for something to wear. It was seven-thirty in the morning and I had a class at nine. I certainly wasn't in the mood for small talk or being lectured.

"How are you and that biker doing? Trevor."

"Fine." Hearing his name made my chest heavy. "Why are you asking?" I asked, pulling out a green cashmere sweater.

"You've been home lately. At night. And, these last two weekends, you didn't even go over to his place."

"I've been busy with homework," I said, not wanting to get into it with her. The truth was that I'd been avoiding him ever since Brandy, his ex-girlfriend, had dropped the bomb about being pregnant. She'd claimed that it was his baby and Trevor, having been abandoned by his mother, and treated so shitty by his old man, wanted to do the right thing for any child he'd fathered. Unfortunately, that also meant allowing her to live in his house, since she "supposedly" didn't have anywhere else to go.

"Everything is good?"

I turned around and looked at her. She'd probably jump for joy if she knew the truth. That we weren't doing well at all. I decided to keep it to myself, however. If things worked out, and the baby wasn't his, she'd still throw it in my face. My mother loved me but she didn't trust or even particularly like Trevor; this would be just more ammunition that she'd use against "The Biker."

I shrugged. "Yeah. Sure. Why are you so worried about it?"

"I'm just worried about *you*," she answered, her green eyes soft. "You've been so quiet. Too quiet."

My stomach began to roll again. "To be honest, I think I have a touch of the flu or something," I replied, making a beeline toward the bathroom again.

"Gerald had it last week, so that's probably it," she replied as I closed the door.

I leaned over the toilet and that alone made me throw up.

"I'll get you some Ginger Ale," she said, through the doorway. "That might settle your stomach."

"Um, thanks, Mom," I croaked.

"You're welcome."

I wiped my mouth with a tissue, dropped it into the toilet, and flushed. As I was brushing my teeth, she knocked on the door again.

"Here, you go," she said, handing me a glass and two pills.

I stared down at them. They weren't anything I recognized. "What are these?"

"Papaya. These will help settle your stomach. Jim uses them all the time for heartburn. You can chew them."

"Thanks," I replied, taking them. "Oh, they're good."

"I know. I've been taking them myself lately." Her eyes went to my stomach and she changed the subject dramatically. "You've been using protection?"

I raised my eyebrow. Not this conversation. I was twenty-one years old and she was grilling me about sex. "Excuse me?"

She laughed nervously. "I'm sure that you are, but... you know." Her face became serious. "You're not pregnant, are you?"

"No, I'm on the pill."

"Oh, good. Have you been using condoms, too? I mean, it's a good idea with a man like Trevor," she said, frowning. "One can only imagine the kind of women he's been with."

"Mom, now you're offending me, too," I said, taking another drink of the Ginger Ale. "And, can we not talk about this? I'm clearly an adult now, and my sex life isn't something I really want to discuss with you."

"I'm just looking out for you," she said, wringing her hands together.

"Fine. Thank you. Now, if you don't mind, I'm going to get dressed and head out to school."

"Can I make you any breakfast?"

The thought of food made me shudder. "No. I don't think I'll be able to keep it down."

Her lips pursed. "If you have the flu, you shouldn't even be going to school."

I pulled out a pair of underwear and a bra from my dresser. "I have a test this morning," I said, slipping my panties on under my white, terrycloth robe. "I can't afford to miss it."

"I'm sure that you can make it up. Tell them you're sick."

She had an answer for everything. "I don't want to make it up. Besides, I'm feeling better. I think that soda you gave me is already helping. Do we have any crackers? I'll take some of those with me."

"Yes. I'll go and put some into a plastic bag for you," she said, walking toward my door. "I'll do it quickly."

"Thanks."

"Of course."

I finished getting dressed and then went back into the bathroom, pulling my hair into a ponytail. I thought about putting makeup on, but then decided against it.

What was the point?

"Here," said Vanda, as I stepped into the kitchen with my backpack. "Saltine crackers."

I took the bag from her. "Thanks."

"By the way, I'm having a late dinner with Jim again tonight. After work. If you need anything, though, call me. I'll come home instead."

"Don't worry about me, I'll be fine," I said, noticing that she'd taken extra care with her auburn hair. Normally, she wore it in a chignon for work, but today, she'd curled it and left it down. "Your hair looks very nice."

She touched it and smiled. "Thanks. Jim likes it this way."

"Ah. I can see why. You two have fun tonight. And, if you decide not to come home, that's fine, too."

"Oh." Waving her hand, she laughed. "I'll be home. We haven't gotten to that point yet."

"Well, when you do, make sure you use a condom," I said, enjoying the sudden embarrassment on her face. "I don't need any little brothers or sisters."

"Goodness, I'm too old to have any more kids," she answered, turning her back to me. She grabbed a bottle of disinfectant and began cleaning the counter.

"Mom, you're not even fifty yet. It could happen," I said, taking the keys out of my purse.

"Just worry about you, Adriana," she said, pulling at the paper towels. She glanced at me over her shoulder. "Okay?"

"The same goes for you, Mom," I said, winking at her. "We're both grown women, right?"

She chuckled and then nodded. "Fine. Point taken."

I smirked. "Finally. I'll see you later tonight."

"Goodbye, Adriana."

I left the house and got into my car. As I pulled out of the garage, my cell phone began to ring. When I noticed that it was Trevor, I swore under my breath and then reluctantly answered it.

"Hey, Kitten," he said in that lazy, sexy voice of his.

"Hi."

"What are you doing?"

"I've got a class. I'm heading to it now."

"Just one?"

"No, three, actually."

"Stop by here when you're done."

I frowned. The last thing I wanted was to see Brandy looking like she owned the place when I arrived. I knew she hated me. I'd seen it in her eyes. She'd do her best to make me feel like I didn't belong there. That was not something I felt like dealing with at the moment. "I... I'm feeling a little under the weather. I'm going to have to pass."

He sighed. "You're avoiding me."

"No."

"Yes you are."

"I'm seriously, not feeling good."

"Right. Just like last week."

"I had classes and tests."

"And the past two weekends?"

"Studying for those tests."

"Fuck, Adriana. This is bullshit. You're avoiding me and it's because of Brandy."

Obviously. "Is she still at your house?"

"Yes, but like I said before, she's just *staying* here. Nothing else is going on. Hell, if I could kick her out today, I would."

"Speaking of – when are you going to find out if the baby is yours?"

"Next week."

I let out a sigh of relief. I'd thought it was going to take much longer for a paternity test. "Do you know how far along she is?"

"Almost nine weeks." He sighed. "Enough about her. I need to see you, darlin'. You don't know how many times I've wanted to drive over to your house and pick you up."

What stopped you? I wanted to ask.

"By the way, I've got something for you," he said, a smile in his voice.

I pictured him holding his crotch and felt myself tingle down below. "Oh yeah? What?"

"No, no, no. It's a surprise. Stop by when you're finished with your classes and you'll get to see."

I relented. "Fine. I should be there around four." I knew that would give me enough time to run back home for a shower and a change of clothes.

"Good. I'll be counting down the minutes. I've missed the fuck out of you, Kitten."

"I've missed you, too." I bit my lower lip. I had to ask. "Is Brandy going to be around?"

"No. I don't think so. She's working at Griffin's now."

I snorted. "Stripping?"

"No, she's taking some bartending classes and Slammer was nice enough to give her a job. She's been training with Misty, too."

"I take it that she got fired from her last job?"

"Yeah. He kicked her out of his house and replaced her at the office."

"What if the baby isn't yours?" I asked. "Do you really want her at Griffin's?"

"I don't care. She needs a job. Besides, I don't spend that much time there, anymore. I usually hang out at the clubhouse."

"Oh, and that's so much better?" I replied, dryly. I still

remembered Krystal telling me about the naked club whores that hung out there. The stripper poles. The booze. From the way she'd explained, it was like a continuous bachelor party that never ended.

"It's not that bad and shit only happens if you want it to happen," he said. "The only thing I want to happen is you in my bed, Kitten. This afternoon."

Although I was still a little nauseated, I wanted it too. I really did miss the hell out of him.

"I'll be there."

TWO

RAPTOR

FTER I HUNG up with Adriana, I walked into the kitchen and brewed some coffee. As I poured myself a cup, Brandy sauntered in wearing a red teddy under a sheer robe that left little to the imagination.

"Oh, I thought you'd taken off already," she said with a coy smile.

Noticing the gleam in her eye, I took a step back. I knew what the hell Brandy was doing – she was wearing the outfit for me, hoping that I'd cave in and fuck her. The girl was a nymphomaniac and although I was pretty horny from not getting laid in the last two weeks, I wasn't about to give in. "I was in the garage, changing oil."

She walked over to the refrigerator, and opened it. "Oh, for your motorcycle?"

"No. Too cold to be riding anything in Iowa but a cage now. I was changing the oil in my truck."

She leaned over, her ass sticking in the air as she searched around for something to eat. "I didn't know you even owned a truck."

I looked away. "Lots of things have changed since we broke up."

She grabbed a jar of pickles and stood up straight. "I guess so."

I turned back and glanced down at the jar. "Pickles for breakfast, huh? You *must* be pregnant."

She put it on the counter and unscrewed the cover. "Yeah, I guess it's true what they say about pregnant women craving pickles," she said, taking the largest one out. She opened her mouth and slid the pickle inside, sucking the juice noisily while she watched for some kind of a reaction from me.

I bit back a smile. I had to give her credit, when she wanted

11

something, she didn't hold back. "I see you're enjoying the hell out of that one."

She winked. "What can I say? I love to suck on things."

Ignoring her comment, I drank my coffee quickly. It was time to leave before she took it a step further, which I knew she would. "Well, there's another jar in the pantry if you need more," I said, walking over to the sink. I turned on the water and rinsed out my cup. "Help yourself."

She came up behind me and slid her hands around my waist. "What if I said I wanted your pickle," she whispered, running her fingers along my zipper.

I stiffened up. "Enough," I muttered, grabbing both of her hands. I turned around and stared down at her. "You've got to stop doing this shit."

"You're hard, Trevor," she said, giving me that old 'come-fuck-me' stare. "You know, if you'd like, I'll take care of it. And, don't worry," she smiled wickedly. "I won't tell if you won't."

"I'm not going there with you. Besides, it's just a reflex," I said, releasing her hands. I moved around her. "Now, go and get some fucking clothes on."

"Trevor, wait," she said, as I headed toward the kitchen door.

Frustrated, I turned around. "What?"

"Are you still seeing her?"

"Her name is Adriana, and yes, I am. I told you before, Brandy, she's my Old Lady now."

She put her hands on her waist. "Then where has she been?" she said, her voice cracking. "I mean, she sure as hell took off when she found out that I was pregnant. Most women would have stayed with their man, even in that circumstance."

"She's confused. It's not every day that I ask a woman to marry me and then thirty minutes later, have her find out that I might be a father to someone else's kid."

"You asked her to marry you?" she croaked, her eyes filling with tears.

I nodded.

"You *never* asked me. I was your Old Lady for two years and not once did you ask me to marry you."

"How do you know that I wasn't going to?" I snapped, remembering a time when I'd been looking at rings. It was around Valentine's Day the year before, and I'd come so close to buying her an engagement ring. But, Slammer had called my cell, ordering me back to the clubhouse. Looks he'd saved me that time, too.

She started to cry. "I'm so sorry, Trevor. Maybe if I'd have known..."

I grunted. "What? You wouldn't have ended up in another man's bed?"

Brandy started in with the familiar apologies and excuses but I cut her off. "I don't want to hear any of this from you," I said, glaring at her. The fuck if she was going to turn this around and try to make me feel guilty. *Me?* "For one, you knew how important you were to me. I patched you. I made you my fucking Old Lady. Would I have married you? Eventually. But, that ship has sailed and we're at the point of no return. The only reason you're living in my house is so that if that kid is mine, I know it has a roof over its head. As far as me and you? Get that shit out of your mind because I'm in love with

Adriana, now."

"Really?" she scoffed "You love her? You barely even know her."

"What the hell does that matter?" I replied. "You and I were together for two years, Brandy, and I didn't fucking know you, either."

"But—"

"Save your excuses," I said, leaving the kitchen. "I'm not interested."

"Trevor!" she hollered, following me.

I turned on my heel and glared down at her. Hearing my birth name coming out of her lips was now even making me mad. "From now on, call me Raptor."

The pained look in her eyes almost made me take it back, but then I remembered what had brought us to that point.

"You're a heartless asshole," she said bitterly.

"I'm heartless?" I grinned coldly. "It's funny how the wheels have turned, isn't it? Look, do us both a favor – you stay out of my way and I'll stay out of yours. Oh, and one more thing…"

Glaring back at me, she raised her chin. "What?"

"Stop walking around this place half-naked. I'm not interested in talking to you or fucking you."

Brandy turned around and stomped into the guestroom. She slammed the door and the entire house shook.

THREE

RAPTOR

A N HOUR LATER, I pulled up to the clubhouse in my Laramie. When Tank noticed me, he opened the gate. I waved and parked my truck next to his older model Silverado.

"I need a new truck," he said, nodding in approval as I locked the door to mine. "You pay that thing off yet?"

"Two more years."

"What are you waiting for, brother? Pay that shit off now," he lectured. "You've got the cash. I know you do. All of that remodeling you did for Brick and his cousin and then those side jobs you've been doing for the old man."

He was right. I'd made a shitload of cash but I knew what I was doing. "It's an interest-free loan. I'd rather keep the money and earn my own interest."

He smirked. "You're such a frugal shopper."

I shrugged. "It pays to know what you're doing, Tank," I said, running a hand through my hair. It was still partly wet and the cold November climate wasn't helping. "I do my research before dropping cash down for any large purchase. You should, too."

He entered the code to get into the building. "I have no patience for the internet or researching 'deals', like you do. That's why I'm dragging your ass with me when I pick out my next truck. Maybe when I get a new bike, too."

"You are replacing yours already? It's only a couple of years old."

"No, just adding to the collection. Got my eye on the V-Rod."

"Sweet. I was looking at them myself. Hey, Cheeks," I said, acknowledging her wave. She was sitting at the bar with another female.

17

"Hey, sexy," said Tank, heading straight for them. "Who's your friend?"

"This is Layla," she said. "My niece. She's only seventeen, so don't even think about hitting on her, Tank."

The teenager, a pretty girl with long, dark hair and brown eyes, blushed and looked away quickly.

"Whatcha bringing her in here for then?" he asked, frowning. "This isn't a place for kids. You of all people should know that."

Cheeks was one of the club whores and proud of it. She specialized in blow jobs and even I had to admit, she could bring a guy to his knees in less than sixty seconds. She opened up her purse and grabbed a pack of cigarettes. "Nothing wild is going on here right now, Tank. Anyway, I brought her in to talk to Slammer."

"Oh yeah?" he said, walking around the bar to the cooler. "About what?"

Cheeks lit the end of her cigarette and took a drag. "Tell him, Layla."

The girl cleared her throat. "I, um, I saw Misty with one of the Devil's Rangers last Sunday."

"Misty?" he said, pulling out a bottle of beer. "The bartender at Griffin's?"

The girl nodded.

"You want one?" asked Tank, nodding to the bottle.

"No, I'm good," I replied, sitting down next to Layla. "Where did you see them?"

"Layla works at a restaurant, about an hour north of here. In Stacy," stated Cheeks. "Jerry's Diner."

"You a waitress there?" asked Tank, watching the girl closely.

She nodded. "Yeah, but I didn't serve them. I recognized her, though."

"I had Misty over a couple of times," said Cheeks. "Card games, you know? Anyway, one time Layla was over and Misty was giving her advice on guys. She was pretty drunk that night. That's probably why she didn't recognize Layla at the diner."

Tank looked at me and then back at Layla. "You sure she was with one of them?"

"Yeah," she replied. "I saw the patches."

"Would you recognize the man if you saw him again?" I asked.

She nodded and then said, "I know his name. His road name."

Tank's eyebrows shot up. "You do? What is it?"

"Mud. The other server said she overheard Misty call him that a couple of times," replied Layla, biting the side of her lip. "He's their president, isn't he?"

Tank and I looked at each other.

"What the fuck? She has no business with Mud," he said, tapping both of his thumbs against the bar.

"That's what I thought," said Cheeks with a sneer. "Sounds like she's up to no good, if you ask me."

"Where's Slammer?" asked Tank, standing up straighter. "He needs to hear this shit."

"Slammer is in back, on the phone," she answered. "He knows we're here to talk about something important. Said he'd be out soon."

"Good," replied Tank.

"Speaking of, I heard you're already planning his bachelor party," I said to him.

Tank nodded. "Yeah. It's in the works. They're eloping in three

19

weeks. December 13th."

"Where they getting hitched?"

"Either Vegas or Hawaii. She wants Hawaii."

"He's never been there, has he?" I asked.

"Hawaii? Just once. After he graduated from high school, his Uncle Shepherd took him out there. As a graduation present. He's been wanting to go back ever since I can remember."

"That was shortly before he joined the Marines and served in Desert Storm, wasn't it?" I asked, remembering the story now.

"Yep. I'm pretty sure they're heading to Maui. He's been looking at vacation packages online."

"You tagging along?" I asked.

"Fuck yeah," he answered, smiling. "You're going, too."

My eyebrows shot up. "Me? I wish I could. I've too much shit going on at the moment. It's not a good time."

"That's why you need to go Hawaii. Leave your troubles behind for a while. Think cocktails, bikinis, sand, and all of us. You'll regret it if you don't fly down there and stay for at least a few days."

I rubbed my chin. "You're right. I should go. I could even take Adriana."

"Or, you could leave her behind," said Tank. "Clear your head of all women for a while."

"Hawaii, huh? I want to go," pouted Cheeks. "I've always wanted to see the volcanos and eat at one of those luaus."

"Sorry, Cheeks," said Tank. "But you don't bring sand to the beach." He turned back to me. "And that's why you should leave yours at home, too. The women out there are supposed to be fuck-tastic."

I smirked. "Fucktastic, huh?"

"Exactly. I'm planning on getting laid the first chance I get, and I'm not talking about those flowers they put around your neck. I'm gonna find me one of those exotic, tight –"

"Okay, we get it," said Cheeks, cutting in.

Layla giggled and Tank gave her a sheepish smile. "Men are all fucking pigs. The sooner you learn the better off you are, Apple Pie."

"Apple Pie?" said Layla, her face turning pink. "I like that."

"There you go, I just found you a nickname," he said, winking. "And if anyone touches you inappropriately in this club, you tell me and I'll beat their ass."

She giggled again. "Okay."

Just then, Slammer walked out of his office and approached us, a grave look on his face.

"What's up?" asked Tank. "You look pissed off."

"I'll tell you about it later," he said, turning to Cheeks. "You said you had something to tell me?"

Nodding, she introduced her niece and then explained what Layla had seen at the diner. When she got to the part about Misty and Mud, a vein in Slammer's forehead began to pulsate.

"That fucking cunt," he growled, slamming his fist on the bar, making both of the girls jump. "I should have known. I should have fucking known."

"Don't be so hard on yourself," I said. "Hell, neither of us knew."

"Yeah, but I had this gut feeling about her, especially after she admitted to banging Breaker. Dammit, she's probably been feeding them information about us all along."

21

"There isn't much she could say," said Tank. "Unless, she's been listening at the door or –"

"Or recording us with some kind of listening device," he cut in, a murderous expression on his face. "In fact." Slammer waved his thumb toward the doorway. "Let's go outside and talk. Now I'm all fucking paranoid."

"What about us?" asked Cheeks. "Can we do anything to help?"

He rubbed a hand over his face and then murmured in a low voice, "Actually, yeah. I need you to get over to Griffin's and keep an eye on her, without Layla, of course."

"Okay," she replied, getting off the barstool.

"And obviously, keep this shit under the table. We don't want her to know that we've caught on yet," he added.

"I understand," said Cheeks. She turned to Layla. "Let's go, hon."

"Wait a second." Slammer's eyes softened. He looked at Layla and pulled out his wallet. "Thanks for the information, sweetheart. Why don't you take this and go buy yourself something pretty."

Her eyes lit up as he handed her three hundred dollars. "Oh, my God, this is really *all* for me?"

Slammer winked at her. "It sure is. Think of it as a reward, and if you ever see any of those assholes in your diner again, give me a call," he replied, handing her a business card.

"I will. Thank you so much, uh, Mr. Slammer."

He chuckled "You can drop the Mister. It's just Slammer."

"Okay," she replied, stuffing the money into her purse. "I'll definitely keep my eyes open for you."

"I know you will." He looked at Cheeks and his smile dropped.

"I appreciate you bringing this message to me. Next time, though, don't bring her here. She's too young for this place."

"Aint nothing going on right now," repeated Cheeks, waving her hand. "It's like a morgue in here."

"It's still early, but that's not the point. If shit was going on and we had a raid of some sort, you don't want your niece involved, you know what I'm saying?"

She sighed and nodded.

"I don't want *any* minors in here. You got that?" he said, looking at us, too.

Nodding, Tank and I looked at each other, a little surprised. I'd noticed that he'd changed considerably after meeting Frannie. The old Slammer wouldn't have cared what age Layla was and he might have even hit on her himself. Obviously, he was getting his own shit together and it made me respect him that much more.

"You want to get together, later this afternoon?" Cheeks asked Tank.

"I don't know. I've got some stuff to take care of," he replied.

"No problem," she smiled. "What about tonight?"

"Maybe. I'll let you know."

She leaned over the bar, slid her arms around his neck, and whispered something into his ear.

He laughed. "How can I say 'no' to that?"

"I was hoping you'd say that. I'll wait for your call," Cheeks said, happy again. Slinging her purse over her shoulder, she turned to Layla. "Let's go, Apple Pie."

The girl giggled. "Okay. It was nice meeting you all."

"You too. Come back when you're legal," called Tank, staring at her ass as she followed her aunt out.

Slammer reached into his pocket and took out a pack of smokes and a lighter. He pulled out a cigarette and shoved it between his lips. "Okay, let's go outside and figure shit out."

Tank guzzled the rest of his beer and we followed Slammer to the back of the building.

"So, what are you going to do?" asked Tank, as we stepped outside.

He lit his cigarette. "First I'm going to get this place checked for bugs."

"Why don't we just interrogate Misty now?" replied Tank. "*Make* her tell us exactly what the fuck is going on."

Slammer blew out a stream of smoke and shook his head. "No. For one thing, Misty might get off on it, the crazy bitch. For another, we might be able to use this to our advantage."

"What do you mean?" I asked, leaning against the door.

"I think we should set 'em up. In fact," he gave us a shit-eating grin. "I think I might know just how to do it."

"Oh yeah? Fill us in," said Tank.

It took him a while to answer. "Let's just say that spying on us is going to send Mud to prison for a very long time, boys."

"Prison. What do you mean?" asked Tank. "I thought I was going to kill the fucker after you were done eloping?"

"Actually, I've been having second thoughts on that," he answered. "The law is watching us closely these days. Killing any of the Devil's Rangers is too risky. I don't want either of you going to jail. I'd rather see Mud behind bars for the rest of his life and knowing exactly who put him there."

"I don't know," he said. "Prison is too easy of a sentence, if you ask me."

"Death is too *quick* of a sentence," countered Slammer. "We need him to rot behind bars for the rest of his life."

"He's right, brother," I answered. "Mud will suffer more behind bars than he would if you killed him. He's made a lot of enemies and some of them are in prison. Life wouldn't be as easy as you might think for a shit-bag like him."

"Maybe," he answered, not looking too convinced. "So, what's the plan?"

"You'll find out soon enough," answered Slammer, flicking his cigarette away. "I need to make some phone calls and get shit rolling. Once I get the ducks in order and everyone on board, I'll fill you in on the details."

"What do you want us to do right now?" I asked as he opened up the door.

"Get Chopper down here to help you look for wires or any other recording devices. I seriously doubt you'll find anything, though. Misty doesn't seem smart enough to set something like that up and keep it running."

"And none of the Devil's Rangers have ever been to this clubhouse?" I asked. We'd had a lot of parties, but Slammer was selective when it came to outsiders. That didn't mean someone couldn't have slipped in during a drunken bash. Especially with the help of Misty.

"Not that we know of," said Tank, as we followed Slammer down the hallway.

"Exactly and that's why you two need to search this place. I'll be back this afternoon. Oh, before I forget, you find out if Brandy's carrying your kid yet, Raptor?"

"Next week," I answered. Just thinking about it left a sour taste in my mouth. I wanted children someday, but not now and certainly not with Brandy. I just wanted her gone.

"You trust her?" he asked.

I laughed. "Are you fucking kidding me? Hell no."

"That's too bad. I was hoping you two were settling down now that she's pregnant. I was also hoping to use her to keep an eye on Misty. But, if you don't trust Brandy, either…"

"I don't even trust that the child she's carrying is mine."

"If it is?" he asked.

"I'll do my duty as a father and make sure I'm in its life. But I'm not getting back with her, no matter how much she wants it to happen."

"You think she got pregnant on purpose?" he asked.

"I don't think so," I replied. "At least, I hope the fuck not."

"I know you're still pissed at what she did, but do you still have feelings for her?" he asked me.

I smirked. "Only bad ones."

"He's got the hots for Krystal's best friend, Adriana," said Tank.

"That's right. The skinny redhead," replied Slammer. "That's the one you were planning on patching before you found out about the kid, right?"

"Things haven't changed. She's my Old Lady already. Just need to make it official."

He put a hand on my shoulder. "Well, looks like you've got your hands full, son."

"Yeah, but it's nothing I can't handle."

"I'm sure you can handle it fine." He looked over at Tank and then back at me. "Of course you know that we have your back, no matter what?"

"I know and I appreciate it," I answered as his cell phone began to ring.

Slammer pulled it out of his pocket. "It's Frannie. I'd better take this. Why don't you drive over to Griffin's and check on Misty," he told me.

"Sure."

"Hey, babe," he said, walking away.

"Can you fucking believe the nerve of that bitch?" said Tank turning back to look at me as I followed him down the hallway. "I mean the more I think about it, the more pissed I get."

"I don't blame you."

He grunted. "Mud killed my fucking girl, man. *Killed* her. I was going to patch Krystal. You knew that."

I nodded.

"He's lucky to be alive. Hell, he shouldn't be alive; now Misty betrays us with that piece of shit? What the fuck?"

"Don't worry, Tank. They're going to pay," I said. We'd run their club all the way out to Hayward, Minnesota for what Mud had done to Krystal, but more needed to be done. I just hoped that whatever Slammer was planning would be a justifiable enough revenge for murdering a woman his son had fallen pretty hard for.

FOUR

ADRIANA

A
FTER MY FIRST class, I had two hours to spare before
my next, so I drove over to a nearby drugstore and picked
up a tube of lipstick and a package of tampons, just in case
my period decided to rear its ugly head. It was due any day and I
knew that with my bad luck, I'd get it before seeing Trevor. As I
turned the corner to the next aisle, I noticed the pregnancy tests lined
up on a shelf, and the hair stood up on the back of my neck. Although
I was on the pill, I didn't always take them on time.

"Relax, you're not pregnant," I mumbled to myself as I looked
at the prices. They were definitely not cheap, but, neither was having
a baby. Before changing my mind, I grabbed a box with two test
sticks, and made my way to the cashier. If I could rule out being
pregnant, it would be one less thing to worry about at the moment.

"How are you today?" asked the woman behind the counter. She
was in her fifties, had short white hair, and a warm, friendly smile.

"Good and you?" I asked.

"Very good," she replied, picking up the pregnancy kit. "Oh,
my. Someone might be a mother soon? How exciting." Her eyes
sparkled. "Is it for you?"

I laughed nervously and then lied, telling her that it wasn't. I
wasn't even sure why I even did it, but somehow, admitting to the
test made me feel irresponsible. Right now, being pregnant would be
devastating. "It's for a friend."

As if she could read my mind, she gave me a sympathetic look.
"Oh, well I'm sure that whatever the outcome is, your *friend* will be
just fine. Children are a blessing."

"Right," I said, digging into my purse for a credit card.

"By the way, if your friend is pregnant, remind her to start taking prenatal vitamins and folic acid. I'm sure her doctor will also recommend it as well," she commented as I handed her the card.

"I'll let her know," I replied, as the line behind me grew. It was quiet and I felt as if all eyes were on me, that they also knew that I was lying and were shunning me for being so careless.

After she finished ringing me up, I dashed out of the store, my eyes lowered, and got into my car. As I headed back to the campus, my cell phone rang. It was Tiffany.

"Hey, girl, how've you been?"

"Fine," I replied. "What about you?"

"Pretty good, actually. Remember Jeremy?"

"Jeremy Stone? The detective?"

"Yeah."

"What about him?"

"We went out on a date last night."

"You did? Wow, how did that go?"

"It was fabulous. He bought me dinner and then we went dancing."

"And then...?" I asked, waiting for her to tell me that she'd screwed his brains out.

"That's it. We have another date planned for Sunday. He has these crazy hours, so we have to wait until then."

"So, you didn't bring him back to your apartment?"

"No. I wanted to, believe me, but he said we should wait before we take that step."

That was a shocker. She'd offered herself to him and he'd

refused? "He's the one who suggested it?"

"Yeah." She giggled. "Wild, huh?"

"He sounds like a decent enough guy," I replied, impressed.

"I think so, too. Anyway, the reason I was calling was to see if you wanted to meet up with me and Amber for dinner tonight? We haven't seen you since Tiffany's funeral and we miss you, dammit."

"I'm sorry but I can't," I replied. "I'm meeting Trevor and then I have all this homework. What about Friday? I miss you guys, too."

She was silent for a few seconds. "Yeah. That might actually be better, anyway. Then Monica can meet up with us, too."

"Sounds great. I'll call you later in the week and we'll plan something."

"Okay. How are you and Trevor, doing, by the way?"

I hadn't told anyone about Brandy being at his house or her being pregnant. They would have told me to kick his ass to the curb. Although I was deeply annoyed about Brandy, I loved Trevor and wanted to be with him. Needed to be with him. I just couldn't fully understand why he had allowed her to move in after everything that had happened. "We're good," I told her.

"Well, leave him at home Friday. It's just going to be us girls. Okay?"

"Sure. No problem."

"I have to go. I'll talk to you soon."

"Goodbye, Tiff."

"Bye."

After she hung up, I actually started feeling better and even a little hungry. Relieved, I purchased a sandwich and a lemonade from the college's cafeteria. Fortunately, I was able to keep it down and the rest of the day went a lot more smoothly. By the time I was finished with the last class, I felt like myself again, which made me feel silly for spending twelve dollars on a pregnancy test when I could have just as easily spent it on a bottle of wine, or even an eyebrow wax. In the end, I decided to return the test as soon as I got my period, which I hoped wouldn't be until after my evening with Trevor.

Thinking about him, I wondered what kind of surprise he had for me.

Maybe Brandy is moving out?

I could only hope.

Trying to remain positive, I turned on the radio and headed home.

FIVE

RAPTOR

WHEN I REACHED Griffin's, Misty and Brandy were both behind the bar in some kind of deep discussion. "What's up?" I asked, stopping next to a couple of familiar faces. It was shortly after two and the lunch rush appeared to have dwindled down to the usual bar-flies, including Horse and Buck.

"Raptor," said Horse, raising a beer to me.

"No work today?" I asked him. He was a mechanic who usually put in over fifty hours a week at his shop, so it was a surprise to see him hanging out at Griffin's on a Monday afternoon.

"I took the day off," he said, the smile on his face receding. "Had to drive my Old Lady to the airport this morning anyway."

"Where's she off to?" I asked, sitting down next to him.

"California. Her sister has cancer and she's going down there for moral support. Fuck, I should have gone with," Horse mumbled, staring at his beer. "I'm an asshole."

"You can still fly out there yourself, can't you?" I asked, looking over his shoulder. "Hey, Buck."

"Hey, Raptor," he answered, barely looking at me. Misty was standing in front of him and leaning over in a way that gave him a great view of her cleavage. She was talking to Brandy about keeping inventory and showing her a checklist.

Horse nodded. "Yeah. She told me I didn't have to go, but I could tell she was just trying to be nice. She knows how busy I am."

"Yeah, you're real fucking busy," laughed Buck, tapping Horse's beer with his.

"Actually, I am," he said, looking serious. "I've got three cages

35

I'm supposed to be working on and look at me. I'm sitting here wasting time. I just…" he rubbed his forehead. "I just felt like such a prick for letting her go by herself. I needed a drink."

"Don't you have other mechanics helping you out?" I asked, remembering him complaining about a couple of them in the past.

"I fired Mikey last week for fucking up one too many times and the other mechanic, Bob, he's doing what he can." He looked at Misty. "Hon, can you pour me a soda. I should probably clear my head and get back down there."

Smiling, Misty grabbed a glass. "Sure, anything for you, Horse. Coke?"

"That'll work."

"What about you, Raptor?" asked Brandy, who was wearing a white camisole under a denim vest that emphasized her fake tits. She put her hand on her hip and smiled seductively. "See anything behind the bar you want?"

"If he doesn't, I sure do," laughed Buck.

"I'll just have what Horse is having," I said, taking out my wallet.

"A soda for you too, huh? Busy day ahead of you?" asked Misty, sliding his over.

"Something like that," I answered, turning around to look at the stage as a popular song from the eighties started, "Hey Mickey." A voluptuous pig-tailed blonde dressed in a cheerleading outfit began shaking her pom-poms and moving to the music.

"I wish she'd blow my mind," said Buck, as the singer shouted the familiar lyrics. He sniggered. "Among other things."

"I should strip," said Brandy, leaning over the bar toward me. She lowered her voice. "Maybe I'd get more of your attention then."

"Don't start," I said tightly, my back to her. "I'm not in the mood."

"What are you even doing here?" she asked, sounding annoyed.

I turned back around. "Checking on things for Slammer. He has some appointments this afternoon and won't be in until later."

"Where's Tank?" asked Brandy. "I'm surprised he isn't here with you."

"He's busy at the clubhouse," I replied, as she filled up a glass of Coke for me.

Misty swung her hair over her shoulder. "Did you say that Slammer has some appointments?"

"Yep," I said, opening up my wallet. I handed Brandy a five dollar bill and she walked over to the register.

"Anything major going on?" asked Misty.

"Major? Like what?"

"I don't know… with the bar? Or any new club recruits?" she asked, grabbing a white towel. She began wiping down the bar with it. "Prospects?"

"You'll have to wait and ask Slammer about it. I know there are some things in the works," I replied, enjoying the way her eyes gleamed after I mentioned the news. I knew that she was probably dying to give out more information to that douchebag, Mud. "Although, it's club business. So he probably won't divulge much to you, darlin'. You know how it is."

"Things in the works, huh? Sounds mysterious. You know what's going on?" she asked Buck.

He burped. "If I knew, you'd have to work harder than that to get it out of me."

37

"I think we both know that I'm quite capable of working *hard*," she replied with a wink.

"Damn, girl. I wish I knew something. I'd let you try to finagle it out of me," he replied, winking back.

I wasn't sure what she may have finagled out of him in the past, but I knew that if Buck was aware of her affiliation with Mud, he'd rather take a bullet than divulge anything else to her.

Misty looked back over at me. "I understand. Business is business and club stuff is club stuff. I'm just an employee and I don't expect to know everything, unless it has to do with my job. I guess I'm just worried about him selling this place."

"He'd better not sell this place," said Horse, frowning. "They've got the best burgers in town."

"Yeah, and not to mention the pie here is phenomenal," said Buck, grinning wickedly.

"Don't worry, if it was something that affected your position here at Griffin's, I'm sure he'd let you know," I answered.

"I'm sure you're right," said Misty.

My phone vibrated; I took it out of my leather jacket and checked the screen. It was Tank.

"What's up?" I asked, turning away from both Misty and Brandy.

"We didn't find any wiretaps or anything else that looked suspicious," he answered. "I think we're good here."

"Chopper's there already?" I asked.

"Yeah, I got ahold of him. He's going to be leaving here shortly, to check Pop's computer and inspect his office at Griffin's. See if there's anything there. Is the bitch there?"

I got up and walked away from the bar. "Yeah, they both are."

"Both? Oh," he laughed. "Brandy."

"Yeah."

He was silent for a few seconds. "Maybe we should go to Misty's place and take a look around before she gets off of work. See if she's got anything on her computer, like emails or other stuff that would give us a clue as to what the fuck she's up to."

Misty didn't seem like the type of person that would spend a lot of time online, but I figured it couldn't hurt to look into it. Especially with Mud living out of state. Hell, maybe they even *Skyped*. "You know where she lives?"

"Yeah. I've been there. I even know where she keeps a spare key."

I walked into the bathroom where it was quieter. "Huh. You sure that she even has a computer?"

"I saw her laptop last spring. She showed me a shitload of nude pictures that someone took of her. I guess she sells them online for extra money."

Someone flushed the toilet, startling me. "Somehow, that doesn't surprise me. Why don't you head on over there, then, and I'll let you know if she leaves here," I said in a low voice as I headed back out of the restroom

"Sounds good."

I hung up and walked back over to the bar.

"Raptor, can you do me a favor?" asked Misty. "We need some beer brought up from the cooler downstairs. Can you grab a few cases?"

I took off my jacket and hung it on the back of the stool. "Sure, what exactly do you need?"

"Actually, I'll come with you. I'd better grab some more vodka and rum, too," she answered, walking around the bar. She looked back at Brandy. "You good?"

"I think I can handle it. We're not exactly busy," she said, nodding toward the tables in front of the stage. There were only a handful of customers, and they were too engrossed in watching the naked stripper do cartwheels.

"See you later," said Horse, standing up. "I'm taking off."

"Me, too," said Buck. "I'm heading over to the clubhouse. Check on things."

"See you guys," said Misty.

"I'll catch you two later," I said, following Misty toward the stairs.

The basement was dark and musty, but cool, so it was a perfect spot to house most of the supplies for the bar. Slammer kept the canned and bottled beer in a large walk-in cooler and I followed Misty inside.

"So, how's she doing?" I asked.

"Brandy? Pretty good. She learns quickly."

"Good."

"She wants you back," said Misty.

"I couldn't care less," I answered, hoping this wasn't going to turn into an attempt to help Brandy.

"I figured, but she's been talking about you so much, it's driving me crazy."

"She drives me crazy, too." I nodded toward the stacked cases of beer. "Which ones do you need?"

She showed me.

"I'll take these up and come back for the rest," I replied, grabbing two cases.

"What's going on with you and that other gal with the red hair?"

"Adriana? She's my Old Lady now."

Her eyebrows shot up. "Does Brandy know that?"

"I told her," I said, walking past her.

"You might want to tell her again," she called behind me.

I grunted. "She only hears what she wants. I told her twice already. I'm done trying to explain shit to her."

"She loves you, you know."

"Fuck that. She doesn't know the meaning of the word," I replied, walking up the stairs. "Now, unless you have a complaint about her that is not related to me specifically, I'd rather not discuss the bitch."

Misty grabbed a bottle of vodka from one of the shelves and laughed. "Okay, I hear you loud and clear. What I don't get is why you're living together."

"You don't have to 'get' it. It's just how things are right now," I replied, glancing back at her over my shoulder.

She looked up at me from the bottom of the stairwell. "Adriana must be pissed as hell. I know I'd be."

"Fortunately, you aren't her," I mumbled to myself, walking away. "Or I'd have to shoot myself."

SIX

BRANDY

AFTER TREVOR FOLLOWED Misty downstairs and Buck left with Horse, I quickly reached into his jacket and pulled out his cell phone. I knew it was wrong, but was curious to find out what exactly was happening between Trevor and Adriana.

As I was scrolling through his text messages, a customer I'd served earlier set an empty glass on the bar. He was in his thirties, clean-cut, and very attractive. As I looked closer, I could see that he had money because of his expensive suit and the Rolex on his wrist.

Hoping for a big tip, I smiled warmly. "Yes?"

"Hey, doll, can I get another drink?" he asked, smiling back.

"Sure," I answered, slipping Trevor's phone into my apron.

"Thanks, just put it on my tab." He sat down at the bar and looked around. "No waitresses to help you out?"

"Most of them don't come in until around four and one called in sick today. I'm all you've got right now," I said, noticing that he had thick lashes, large puppy-dog brown eyes, and a dimple that made him that much cuter.

"Don't get me wrong, beautiful. I'm not complaining. If you're all I have then as far as I'm concerned, it's my lucky day," he flirted, his eyes dropping to my cleavage. "Hell, I'd rather watch you pour drinks than look at what's on stage right now."

Enjoying the attention, something I'd been trying to squeeze out of Trevor, I giggled at this man's boldness. "Thanks. You're very sweet. What can I get you?"

"A rum and Coke. Please."

I quickly mixed a drink and slid it over to him just as Trevor stepped back behind the bar. He set down two cases of beer and without even a glance in our direction, turned around, and went back toward the basement.

"What's your name?" asked the guy in the suit.

"Brandy. What's yours?"

"My name is Jake. Brandy, huh?" he asked, stirring his drink. "Is that your real name?"

I nodded. "Mom had a weakness for it in her younger years. Anyway, I used to hate the name, but now I kind of like it."

"You should. It's nice. 'Brandy' feels good on the tongue," he said, his eyes holding mine.

I smirked. "It does, huh?"

"Definitely."

"So, what's your wife's name? Is it something that feels good on the tongue, too?" I asked, nodding toward the ring on his left hand.

His smile fell. "It used to. Now I have a hard time even saying her name."

I had been hit on by several married men in the last few days. I didn't mind at all, they usually tipped better, especially if I laid on the charm. I could tell that this guy was about to use the "Woe is me; my wife is a bitch" card. I could feel it coming. "What is it?"

"Cara," he said, looking away.

"Will she be joining you soon?"

Jake laughed grimly. "You mean *here*?"

"Yeah. Some couples get off on watching each other getting lap dances. We also get a lot of swingers in here. I've seen it all."

"Is that right?" he said, taking a sip of his drink. "Well, these days she only gets off by fucking my brother."

Surprised by his response, I sucked in my breath . "No. Are you serious?"

He snorted. "I wish I wasn't."

"When did you learn about them having an affair?" I asked, now feeling sorry for him. I could tell that he was being sincere. There was nothing fake about the pain in his eyes. It was real.

"I've known about it for only a couple of days."

"Have you confronted her?"

"No. Not yet. She's been away on business."

"What about your brother?"

"He's away on business." He grunted. "With her."

"You must be so angry at the both of them," I said, shocked at how calm he was being. When I cheated on Trevor, he'd punched everything but me and even that had taken a lot of restraint.

"I am but the truth is, we'd been having problems in our marriage before she started messing with my brother."

"Really?"

"Yeah. I wanted to have a baby and she thinks that kids are a waste of time and money."

"Wow."

"Yeah. Wow. Anyway, things went from bad to worse right after my mother died."

I put a hand to my heart. "Your mother died, too? I'm so sorry for your loss. You've really had a horrible time of it, haven't you?"

"It's been tough," he said, staring past me at the liquor bottles behind the bar. "After she died, my wife started spending a lot of time with my brother, who seemed to be taking Mom's death harder than any of us. They'd been closer, though. I get it. Anyway, I thought it was odd that my brother and Cara were spending so much time together. I had no idea that they were fucking, though. Talk about a slap in the face."

"That's horrible," I agreed. "I just can't believe she did that to you. Or, your brother for that matter. How could they?"

"I know. I'm still trying to come to grips with everything. What really goads me is that my brother and I are twins. We used to be so close and now this. I don't know what I'm going to do."

I stared at him in shock. "He's your twin?!"

Jake nodded.

I reached over and laid my hand over his. "I'm sorry to hear about your wife and brother. You're good looking and seem very sweet. I'm sure you'll meet someone else. Someone who appreciates you."

"I hope so. I've been so lonely these past few months. And," he looked embarrassed. "This may sound pathetic, but it's been so long since I've seen a naked woman. It's why I chose this place for a drink."

"You poor guy. Here," I said, grabbing the bottle of rum. I began pouring him another drink. If anyone needed to get wasted, it was him. "Have one on me."

He smiled warmly. "You're a breath of fresh air, Brandy. I haven't had a woman treat me so nicely in quite a while. Especially one so beautiful."

My cheeks grew warm. It was nice getting a compliment from a good-looking man. Especially one who stared at me with appreciation. Trevor now only looked at me because he had no other choice. Of course, I understood why he was pissed at me. I'd fucked up by cheating on him. As far as I was concerned, however, I deserved a second chance. He was being so damn stubborn.

"You're so sweet," I said straightening up. Wanting to make him feel better, I tossed my blonde hair over my shoulder and looked him square in the eye. "Your wife has really fucked up."

"Thanks. I like to think so, too."

Misty and Trevor stepped back to the bar.

"You need anything else?" asked Trevor, setting down two more cases of beer.

"Actually," replied Misty. "I hate to ask this of you, but we're running low on glasses and the busboy called in sick about an hour ago. Since we're so short-staffed, maybe you could help us out by doing some of them?"

Trevor nodded toward me. "Have her do some dishes. She's the one getting paid to work here."

Misty shook her head. "She needs to help me tend the bar."

Before he could protest, the front door opened up and four guys walked in.

"See, we have more customers and Happy Hour should be starting soon. Just help us out and wash a few glasses, please?" asked Misty.

Trevor sighed. "Fine. I'll do some." He grabbed his leather jacket and headed toward the kitchen.

"Thanks, Raptor," Misty hollered.

He raised his thumb and disappeared into the back.

"Raptor, huh?" asked Jake. "Is that his Road name?"

I nodded, surprised that he knew the term. "He's part of the

Gold Vipers Motorcycle Club."

"Huh," he replied, staring toward the kitchen.

"You've obviously heard of them," I said, watching as Misty walked over to the table of newcomers.

He nodded. "I'm a lawyer. I've definitely heard of the name."

My eyes widened. Lawyers intrigued me. "You're a lawyer? That's so cool."

Jake smiled in amusement. "I'm a Defense Attorney," he said, handing me his business card. "It's not always as cool as you'd think."

I stared down at it. "I don't know. I think that's so impressive. That you're a lawyer. You must have gone to school for a long time."

"It took a while," he said, removing his suit jacket and placing it on the back of the stool. "But, well worth it."

I slipped his card into my apron and watched as he loosened his tie. Besides being successful and cute, he had broad shoulders and a narrow waist. In all accounts, he was yummy.

"So, when do you get off of work?" he asked, noticing that I was staring at him.

"In four more hours," I replied, surprised that he was asking. "Why?"

"I was just wondering if you'd be interested in joining me for dinner."

I smiled. "I... I don't know."

"It's just dinner," he said, giving me another dimpled grin. "I suppose you have a boyfriend? A beautiful woman like you usually does."

"I don't, actually," I replied softly.

"That's a relief. I was hoping you'd say that."

"I can't go to dinner with you, though."

"Why?"

I looked back toward the kitchen. As tempting as it was to go out with Jake, I still wanted Trevor back and if he found out about it, that would put even more distance between us.

"I just can't."

Jake looked wounded. "Okay."

"Not that I don't want to," I said, smiling at him. "Believe me, I do. I just… I have some issues in my life that need to be resolved before I can decide to do something like that."

"I understand. Issues are my middle name, right now." He finished his drink and stood up. "I'll be right back. Where is the men's room?"

"It's over there," I said, pointing. "Down that hallway and to the left."

"Thanks."

I watched him go and felt like such a heel. He seemed like a nice guy and could probably use some female companionship. Especially since his wife and brother had screwed him over like that. If that wasn't bad enough, he'd made it pretty clear that he hadn't had sex in a while and it seemed like such a waste. Hell, I hadn't had sex in a while and that was bad enough.

A wicked thought flitted through my head and my sex twitched in excitement.

I bet we could help each other out, I thought, imagining us fucking in one of the back offices or even the alleyway. I pictured his hands all over my body as he impaled me with whatever was hiding under his trousers and I could feel my panties get wet.

"Fuck it," I mumbled, deciding to throw caution to the wind and go for it. I was tired of my vibrator and needed a real man to give me what I needed. Something told me that Jake would definitely give it to me and without any strings attached.

I turned to Misty, who was back at the bar. I touched my temple and winced. "Hey, um, I know you need me but would you mind if I took a quick break? I've got this splitting headache and I think that if I take a couple of pills and just chilled out for a while, I'll feel much better."

"No problem. I can handle it," said Misty, her eyes sympathetic. "Go ahead and get away for a few minutes. The music probably isn't helping your headache."

"No, it's not. Thanks. I'll be back soon."

"Okay."

I walked away from the bar and turned the corner, to stand next to the men's bathroom. When Jake stepped out, he stopped abruptly. "Are you waiting for me?" he asked, pleasantly surprised.

"Yeah, actually I am. I have this problem and I think that you might be able to help me out with it," I said, grabbing his hand.

"A problem?" he answered, looking unsure as she dragged him toward Slammer's office. "What sort of problem?"

I opened the door and pulled him inside. Then I locked it and turned around. "I guess that you could say it's the same one that you're having right now, too."

He looked confused. "You've lost me. What kind of a problem am I having?"

I grabbed him by the belt and pulled him toward me. "You need to get laid. So do I."

His eyes widened at the touch of my hand on his crotch, which was now as hard as a rock.

"That feels nice. We don't have much time," I whispered, unbuckling his pants. I stopped abruptly and looked up at him. "I'm sorry, are you okay with this?"

Jake, who was staring at me in wonder, pulled me into his arms. "That's an understatement," he said, before crushing his lips against mine.

THREE MINUTES LATER, Jake had me bent over Slammer's desk.

"Do it harder," I demanded, looking at him over my shoulder. "Fuck me harder."

Jake increased his thrusts and I gasped in pleasure as he hit my G-spot. Getting fucked in Slammer's office by a stranger with a big cock, was so exciting that I came within seconds.

"Yes," I growled, clenching my teeth together as he kept going. After a few more thrusts, he gasped in pleasure and pulled out of me, squirting his seed all over my back.

"Fuck," he whispered, wiping his forehead with the back of his hand. "Did that just happen?"

"I know, right?" I whispered, turning around to look at him. "I just wish we had more time to go again."

"Yeah, me too. Sorry, I couldn't last. Like I said, it's been a while and you're so damn sexy." He grabbed a couple of tissues from Slammer's desk and began wiping my back off with them. "So, who's Trevor?"

"What do you mean?" I asked, feeling my cheeks turn red.

"You said his name once."

I'd noticed it too but had hoped he'd missed it. "I'm sorry. It's my ex, but, I swear, it was a reflex," I lied. "I knew exactly who was fucking me."

Jake threw the tissues away. "It's okay. I won't hold it against you. I've got my own issues. You certainly helped me forget them for a while, though."

"Glad I could help." The phone inside my apron began to buzz. "Oh, shit," I said, realizing that I still had Trevor's phone. I pulled it out and noticed that Tank had been trying to call him. I needed to get his phone back inside of his jacket before he found that it was missing.

"Everything okay?"

I nodded. "We need to sneak out of here, though. Why don't you go first?"

He kissed me and then quietly slipped out of the office.

I checked Trevor's phone again to see if anyone else had tried calling. It was then that I noticed an outgoing call. One that had occurred within the last few minutes.

I covered my mouth. "Oh, my God."

Apparently, I'd accidently called Adriana during my session with Jake. The call had actually lasted for almost two minutes and I wondered if Adriana had heard anything. If Adriana *had* she would definitely think that it was Trevor having sex with another woman. It would end their relationship.

Grinning triumphantly, I erased the call, to cover my tracks. Alive with excitement, I snuck out of Slammer's office and went back to the bar, singing to myself.

"You must be feeling better," said Misty, pouring a drink for Jake. "Headache gone?"

I nodded quickly. "Yeah. It's much better. Is Trevor still doing dishes?"

"Raptor? Yeah, I think so," she answered.

"Okay," I replied, walking over to where the glasses were kept behind the bar. "I'll go back and get some. We're really getting low."

"Good idea."

I went to the kitchen and spotted Trevor by the sink, loading the last of the dirty glasses into the large dishwasher. He had his hair pulled back into a ponytail and wore a black doo rag.

"What's up?" he asked, glancing at me.

"I'm just checking to see if you have some clean ones ready yet."

He nodded toward a crate of glasses. "Those are clean."

"Okay," I said, noticing his jacket, which was slung over a metal chair, a few feet from the sink. "Oh, do we have any more Bloody Mary mix? I should bring some out."

"It's in the cooler," he said, nodding toward a pair of metal doors.

I laughed nervously. "Could you get it for me? I saw a mouse in there last week. It freaked the hell out of me."

"A mouse in the cooler?"

I nodded.

Sighing, Trevor turned off the water and marched over to the cooler. When he was inside, I quickly rushed over to his jacket and slipped the phone back into one of the pockets. As I was moving away, he walked out of the cooler with two bottles of Clamato. "Will this work?"

"Yeah, thanks," I replied, as he handed it to me. "I owe you."

Not answering, Trevor walked back over to the sink and began washing dishes again.

"You okay?" I asked, noticing the way his jaw was set.

He wiped his forehead with the back of his hand. "I'm fine. Misty still out there?"

"Yeah, where else would she be?"

His phone began to ring and I jumped.

"Someone's a little jittery today," said Trevor walking over to his jacket. He pulled out his phone and looked at the screen.

"Who is it?"

"Tank," he replied and then answered the phone.

I listened as he talked with Tank, my heart pounding wildly in my chest.

"What do you mean you've been trying to call me? My phone hasn't rang in the last half hour," said Trevor. "Seriously, brother. I haven't heard it ring."

Swallowing, I turned around and quickly left the kitchen.

SEVEN

ADRIANA

I STARED AHEAD IN horror as the sounds of the couple having sex made me want to throw up. I recognized the woman's voice right away – it was Brandy's, and the name she'd cried out had gutted me.

Trevor.

I hung up the phone and threw it across my bedroom, crying. The realization of what was happening seemed to hurt worse than anything I'd encountered in the past. Even the death of my father and best friend seemed to be overshadowed by the heart-wrenching pain I was feeling at the moment.

How could he do this to me?

I crawled into my bed, curled up into a ball, and sobbed. There was no doubt in my mind that Brandy's baby was Trevor's and that he'd lied about everything. My mother had been right about him from the very beginning. The man was nothing but a despicable pig and I vowed to never trust anything that came out of his mouth ever again.

EIGHT

RAPTOR

"**Y**OU FIND ANYTHING?" I asked Tank, still wondering why I hadn't heard my phone go off. After looking at the call log, I'd found he'd been right. He'd definitely tried calling me more than once. I decided to contact my cell phone provider and rip them a new one. Something was obviously wrong and it was usually their fault.

"Yeah. That's why I've been trying to call you. We've learned a lot of shit. Get a load of this – Misty wasn't only fucking Breaker, but she was his Old Lady."

My eyes widened. "What?"

"Yeah. Apparently, they'd hooked up after he got out of prison. We found some emails from her to both Breaker and Mud."

"Why the fuck was she working for Slammer then?" I said, thinking that Misty was even nuttier than we'd imagined.

"Isn't it obvious? She's the rat we've been trying to flush out all along. Obviously she was working for us before Breaker died, to get information, and now she's doing it for revenge. From the sound of her emails to Mud, the woman is looking for vengeance and will do whatever it takes to get it."

I could hear Misty laughing all the way into the kitchen and it made my blood boil. "You tell Slammer yet?"

"Yeah, he's pissed off but didn't seem too surprised by what we'd found."

"What do we do now?"

"He said he's working on it. Just watch yourself around that sneaky whore."

"Definitely. What about the others? What should we tell them?"

"Nothing. They might fuck everything up if they know what's going on."

"Good point." The others meant well but some of them didn't handle their liquor too well. If Misty got them drunk enough, she could pry anything out of them.

"I can't believe that bitch has the audacity to come in here and pull this shit," I said in a low voice.

"No shit. As far as I'm concerned, she's just as responsible for Krystal's death as Mud. She wants vengeance? She's going to fucking get it. *Mine*. I'm all in this time, brother. Heads are going to roll."

"I'm behind you, man. Whatever you and Slammer need me to do, I'm in, too. No questions asked."

"I appreciate it," he said and then sighed. "I just hope he comes up with something soon because I don't know how much longer I can keep my cool. Especially now that we know what's up."

"No shit. I'd love to grab her by the hair, drag her out outside, and kick her ass to the curb."

"I'd like to do more than that," he mumbled.

"I'm sure you would. You on your way out here now?"

"Yeah. We should be there in about ten minutes or so."

"Okay. See you soon."

After we hung up, I finished up the dishes and walked back into the bar.

"Thanks for doing those," said Misty, when she noticed me. "You saved the day."

"No problem," I answered, as cool as a cucumber. "Anything

for Slammer's customers."

"You work up an appetite yet?" she asked. "Benny should be in soon. He starts at four."

Benny was the short-order cook and made the best burgers in town. Most people stopped in for his food even more so than for the strippers. "Actually, I'm not sticking around. As soon as Tank gets here, I'm heading out."

"Where are you off to?" asked Brandy, walking over to us.

"Got some shit to do. What time are you finished here?" I asked.

"Six."

"You coming straight home?"

"I was planning on it." Her eyes narrowed. "Why?"

"Adriana is coming over," I replied, opening up my wallet. I took out a fifty dollar bill. "Why don't you go to a movie or have dinner with one of your friends?"

"Oh, I get it – you don't want me around when your 'Old Lady' comes over," she said, her tone dripping with scorn.

"It would make things less awkward."

For Adriana. I couldn't care less, myself.

"Why is it so 'awkward', when there's nothing going on between us?" she asked, shoving the money into the front pocket of her jeans.

"You know why, so quit being a fucking smartass," I said, pulling the phone out of my jacket pocket. "Now, can you just give us some time alone? I'm only asking for a couple of hours."

"Sure," she said. "Are you calling her right now?"

"I'm thinking about it." I looked up. "Why?"

"Just wondering."

"Hey, Brandy, can you go and serve that table over there?" asked Misty as two new customers sat down. "While I go and have a quick smoke?"

"Sure."

They both walked away and I called Adriana, wanting to hear her voice again. It bothered me that she'd been trying to avoid me the last couple of weeks, and yet, I'd allowed her to do it. That was my mistake and I wasn't about to let it happen again, even if Brandy was pregnant with my child. Regardless of the outcome, Adriana was part of my future and the hell if I'd let anything come between us.

The phone went to voicemail. I left her a message and then a text, telling her how excited I was to see her later.

NINE

ADRIANA

I STARED AT THE text message from Trevor and it made me so furious, I wanted to break something.

I can't wait to see you, Kitten. I've been thinking about you all day long.

"Not *all* day," I said between clenched teeth. "You lying asshole."

I held the phone firmly in my hand, debating on whether or not to call Trevor or just confront him face-to-face. I wanted to see his expression when I told him off, but I was also a little fearful. Fearful that he'd make a scene or try manipulating me into believing that he'd slipped up and would never do it again. That it had only happened during a moment of weakness between him and a woman he'd once loved.

"Screw that. I'm not to give you another chance," I growled, dialing him back. I would say what I had to say and then hang up, not even giving him a chance to come up with an excuse.

"Trevor," I said firmly, when he answered.

"Hey," he said, a smile in his voice. "I'm glad you –"

"Listen to me," I snapped, my hands shaking so much I could barely hold on to the phone. "I heard you earlier. I heard you fucking her and I don't want you to ever come near me or call me again."

He didn't say anything for a few seconds. "Wait, what are you talking about?"

"You know exactly what I'm talking about. You apparently dialed me by accident when you were fucking Brandy less than an hour ago."

"What? Fucking *Brandy*?" he said, raising his voice. "What the

65

hell are you talking about?"

I laughed coldly. "Like you don't know. I heard you two! I heard her screaming your name as you banged the hell out of her."

"Adriana, I don't know what you're talking about. For one, I would never bang or fuck Brandy. For two, I love *you* and I would never screw you over like that. For three, I've been in the kitchen at Griffin's doing dishes. Why are you – "

Rolling my eyes, I cut in. "Oh, you're good. You're really good. I'm finished with you and all of your fucking lies, so save your excuses."

"Adriana – "

"Stay away from me, Trevor. I mean it this time!" I shouted and then hung up.

He tried calling me back, but I ignored it.

Wiping the tears from my eyes, I grabbed my car keys and left the house. There was a strong chance that he'd rush over and try to talk to me. Beg for mercy. Lie his pants off. I wasn't about to give him the chance.

TEN

RAPTOR

S TILL STUNNED AT Adriana's accusations, I tried calling her back, but she didn't answer. Enraged, I turned around and slammed my fist into the wall.

"You okay?" asked Misty, hurrying over to where I was standing.

"Do I *look* okay?" I growled, turning to stare at Brandy, who was watching me from behind the bar. Her eyes were filled with fear and something in my gut told me that she knew more about what was going on than I did.

"Your knuckles are bleeding," said Misty, holding out a white towel.

I ignored her and stormed over to where Brandy was cowering.

"What's up?" she asked, trembling.

"You. In the back room. Now," I ordered.

She grabbed a glass and filled it with ice. "I was just making a drink for a customer. I can't."

"I don't fucking care what you were doing," I snapped. "I need to talk to you. Now."

"Calm down, pal," said a man wearing a monkey suit, his tone condescending. "You're causing a scene."

Now even angrier that this guy was putting his nose in business that didn't concern him, I shot the stranger a venomous look. "Stay the fuck out of it, *pal*," I spat, almost hoping that he wouldn't. The rage and adrenaline pumping through my veins craved a fleshy outlet. I wouldn't touch Brandy, but the stranger would do just fine. "This doesn't concern you."

"Is this your ex?" asked the man, staring at Brandy now.

She smiled weakly.

"I can see why you're no longer together," he said and turned to Misty. "Misty, right? Where's the bouncer? I think someone needs to make sure this guy doesn't hurt anyone."

"Keep your fucking mouth shut and that won't happen," I said, cracking my knuckles.

"Don't threaten me. I'm a lawyer."

I rolled my eyes. "La-di-fucking-da." I turned away from him. "Brandy, get your ass in back. We need to talk."

"Settle down, Raptor," said Misty. "He's right. You're causing a scene, which usually only happens at night. You're freaking people out."

Before I could respond, the front door opened and Tank stepped into the bar with Chopper.

"Thank God," mumbled Misty, sighing in relief.

I turned back to Brandy. "I'm not fucking around here. We need to talk. Either we do this in the back or I'll embarrass the shit out of you out here. Your choice."

"Fine. I'm coming," she huffed. Brandy looked at Misty. "Can you finish that guy's drink? The one with the glasses at the end of the bar. He wants a gin and tonic."

"No problem. If he decides to stay," she answered, looking amused.

"Hey, brother," said Tank, walking up to me. He arched his eyebrow. "What's going on? You look like you're about ready to kick some serious ass."

"I don't know what's going on and that's the problem," I said, waving to Chopper who was heading toward Slammer's office.

"It have anything to do with what we were talking about earlier?"

"No," I said. "It has to do with Brandy." I looked at her again.

"Let's go. Break room."

"You don't have to talk to me like that," she mumbled, heading toward it. "I'm not a fucking dog."

She was right about that. Dogs were loyal.

ELEVEN

MUD

"YOU SURE ABOUT that?" asked the president of the Devil's Rangers.

"Sure as shit," said the voice on the phone. "Slammer hired The Judge for the job."

"I thought it might be something like that." He closed his eyes and rubbed the bridge of his nose. "And you say that he's related to Raptor?"

"They're half-brothers. His real name is Jordan Steele."

"How'd you get this information?"

"Let's just say that their mother, Mavis, can't handle her liquor. She's in town and made a new friend last night at Sal's."

Sal's was a dive bar in Jensen, frequented mostly by junkies, dealers, and hookers.

"Do you know how to find him?"

"The Judge?"

"Yeah."

"I might. Are you sure you *want* to find him?"

The truth was he wasn't. But, he'd already lost so much and needed to re-establish his reputation. At the moment he looked like a fucking coward. "He killed Breaker. I need to avenge his death."

"Yeah, but do you really think that you can take him out yourself? He's not an easy guy to kill. You've heard the stories."

The Judge was an exterminator. An assassin. A lone wolf. He had a flawless reputation for not only getting the job done, but never leaving a shred of evidence. There were only a handful of people who knew that he even existed. At least that had been the case before Mavis opened her yap. As far as Mud was concerned, this would be

The Judge's undoing.

"I've heard the stories but he's just a fucking guy. One who bleeds like the rest of us," he said.

His informant chuckled. "That's just it, you try fucking with him and you might be the one bleeding."

Mud pulled out a cigarette. "Not if I go after him first. Or send someone else. Hell, I'll turn the shit around and put *him* on a hit list."

There was a long pause. "He's already got a bounty on his head. A big one."

"I figured as much. How much is it?" he asked, lighting his smoke.

"A million."

He coughed. "Really? And nobody has killed him yet?"

"There have been several attempts. One guy who went after him was found hanging from a bridge. Another was left on the front lawn of the person offering the reward. I can't believe you haven't heard the stories."

"I've got my own shit to worry about. No time to listen to gossip. So, who's the guy offering the reward?"

"Some big shot politician whose son was murdered by The Judge."

"What's his name?" asked Mud.

He told him.

"He's a senator, or something, isn't he?"

"Yeah."

"I remember hearing that story on the news last year. Didn't they think it was a car-jacking?"

"No, that's what they wanted the public to believe. Rumor has it that the prodigy son was into child porn. For obvious reasons, the senator didn't want the information leaked. Anyway, it may have looked like a car-jacking gone wrong, but it was a hit. Dad found out and now has a vendetta against The Judge."

"He still paying?"

"The politician?"

"Yeah."

"I believe so."

Mud took a long drag from his cigarette and blew out ring of smoke. "I think I know how to draw this bastard out."

"The Judge?"

"Of course."

"How?"

"His brother. Raptor."

"I don't think they're a very close-knit family," replied the man, sounding amused.

"Maybe not but I'll bet he knows how to get ahold of him."

"Even if he does, I doubt Raptor will divulge such information to you."

"He will if I have something of his. Something worth value."

"Like what?"

Mud grinned. "His Old Lady."

TWELVE

RAPTOR

"I DON'T KNOW WHAT you're talking about," said Brandy after I gave her the third degree. She crossed her arms under her chest. "Obviously Adriana is mistaken or just looking for an excuse to break up with you."

"She doesn't play games like that. Where's your phone?"

Her eyes widened. "In my purse. Why?"

"I want to check your calls."

"Really? You think I'd stoop to something like that?" she snapped, looking upset.

"I don't know, Brandy, but Adriana is angrier than hell and I need to find out what the fuck is going on."

"I don't even have her number."

I ignored her. "Where's your purse."

She raised her chin. "Fine, you want to see my phone? It's under the bar. When you don't find anything on it, I expect an apology."

I walked out of the break room and headed back to the bar. "Misty, where's Brandy's purse?"

"Wait a second, *I'll* get it," said Brandy, walking around me. She stepped behind the counter and kneeled down, out of eyesight.

Frustrated, I leaned over the bar and noticed that she was checking her phone. "What the fuck? Give it to me. *Now.*"

Mumbling under her breath, she stood up and handed it over. "Go ahead. I've got nothing to hide."

I took her phone and scrolled through both the call log and her text messages. I couldn't find anything suspicious, but it wasn't enough to satisfy me. She could have erased an outgoing call.

77

"What's going on?" asked Tank, who was walking toward me from Slammer's office.

I handed Brandy back her phone. "Adriana received a phone call earlier. One that apparently set her off," I replied.

"From Brandy?" he asked.

"I didn't call her," she protested. "I don't have her number and even if I did, I wouldn't waste my time. I've got better things to do with my life."

Like ruining mine, I thought bitterly.

"Why is Adriana so pissed off?" he asked, when Brandy stormed away from us.

"She thought she heard two people having sex, one of them being me."

Tank's eyebrows shot up. "Why did she think it was you?"

I went over our conversation and how she'd freaked out, telling me that she never wanted to see me again.

He sat down at the bar. "Does someone have your phone?"

"No," I answered, pulling it out. "It's been in my jacket all day."

"Did you check your outgoing calls?"

"Tank, I didn't call her," I said, showing him my own call log. "And I haven't had sex in over two weeks."

"What the hell is wrong with you?" he asked, now grinning.

"It hasn't been by choice."

He looked at Brandy, who was bending over by the glasses and re-stocking them. "You're really not tapping that?"

Grunting, I shoved my phone back into my jacket. "Fuck no. Been there. Done that. Won't go back."

He turned back to me. "Better go find Adriana then and set her right. If you've been keeping your dick clean for the past couple of weeks, it must be love."

"I'm going to head out right now and try to talk to her. You need anything from me?"

"No," he answered, lowering his voice. "Chopper is checking the Old Man's office for wiretaps and I'm going to keep an eye on Misty. Go do what you got to do, brother."

"Thanks," I said, grabbing my jacket. As I threw it on, I noticed the guy with the suit eyeballing me, a sneer on his face. I walked over to him. "You gotta problem?"

He grunted. "I think you've already proved who has the problem."

I shook my head and sneered. "Why don't you go and mind your own fucking business?"

"I was trying to until you started hassling Brandy. Someone had to say something."

Even though I was pissed off, I couldn't really blame him for wanting to stand up for her. From an outsider's perspective, I probably looked like an asshole picking on a beautiful girl. It was just unfortunate that she was also a lying, deceitful whore. "You know nothing about Brandy and as far as hassling her, she fucking deserves it. If you knew anything about her, you'd understand."

He picked up his drink. "Oh, I think I know her better than you think."

"I doubt it. You wouldn't be defending her if you did."

He didn't say anything.

"Look, do yourself a favor and stay away from her. You have no idea what kind of a woman she is or the trouble that she brings."

"Thanks, but from where I'm sitting, your advice seems pretty biased."

I looked at Brandy who was staring at us, an unreadable expression on her face. "So is yours, and that's only because you don't know her like I do. Hell, I take that back, nobody knows Brandy. Not even Brandy."

"I doubt that. She seemed pretty stable to me," he said, staring at her appreciatively.

"You said you were a lawyer, huh?"

"I'm a Defense Attorney."

I grunted. "Waste of my fucking time," I said, walking away. Not only did he obviously want to fuck Brandy, he was paid to argue away the facts and defend the guilty. Talking to him was like talking to a wall.

THIRTEEN

RAPTOR

I DROVE OVER TO Adriana's place but nobody was home. I tried calling her phone again, but she continued to ignore me. Frustrated, I decided to try her at work, so I headed over to Dazzle. When I stepped inside, Adriana's mother, Vanda, looked startled.

"Mrs. Nikolas," I said, forcing a smile on my face.

She excused herself from the customer she was talking to and approached me.

"Do you know where Adriana is?"

"No. I haven't spoken to her since this morning." Her face darkened. "Why, what's wrong?"

"Nothing."

She stared into my face and frowned. "Your eyes say different. Are you two fighting?"

Not wanting to get into it with her, I ignored her question. "Could you have her call me? I really need to speak to her."

"Have you left her a message on her phone?"

I nodded.

"Then, she'll call you back when she wants."

"Everything okay here?" asked the security guard, who'd been watching us from a stool near the front of the store.

"Everything's fine. I was looking for Adriana. You're Jim, aren't you?" I asked, remembering that Adriana had mentioned him. Apparently he was dating her mother.

"Yes. You must be Trevor?" he said, his face relaxing. He held out his hand. "I don't think we've been formerly introduced."

I shook it. "No, we haven't. Nice meeting you."

"You as well. So, you're looking for Adriana?"

"Yeah." I turned to Vanda. "I'll swing back over to your place and try to catch her. I stopped there first before driving out here. We may have just missed each other."

"Maybe."

"Well, see you around," I said, turning to leave. As usual, Vanda made me feel like an outsider. It was obvious that she would never accept me or my world.

"Wait, Trevor," said Vanda.

I turned back around.

She sighed. "Adriana wasn't feeling well this morning. I thought that maybe she had the flu."

"Really? I spoke to her earlier but she didn't mention anything about being sick," I replied.

"She was. I'm not even sure why she went to school today. She's stubborn, that one."

Jim laughed. "What do you expect, she's *your* daughter, Vanda."

She smiled weakly. "This is true."

"Thanks," I replied. "I'll leave her alone and let her sleep then."

"That is probably the wisest thing to do."

Nodding, I left the store, hoping that maybe Vanda was finally warming up to me. Now, I just needed to find Adriana and find out what was causing her to be so fucking cold.

FOURTEEN

BRANDY

AFTER TREVOR LEFT Griffin's, Jake tried flirting with me again, but this time I ignored his advances. The quickie in the back had helped with my need to get laid, but I decided that I just wasn't interested in hooking up with him again, especially now that Adriana believed that Trevor had cheated on her. It wouldn't be long until I had him back in my arms and Adriana would be another bump in the road for the both of us. I believed that we were meant to be together and that this part in our lives would only make us stronger in the future.

"So, what was that all about with you and Raptor?" whispered Misty, when Tank left us to go into the back room. "He was flipping out."

"Just a misunderstanding."

"Seemed more than that to me. He was so pissed off that he almost broke his hand punching the wall."

"I know. He has a temper. In fact, he's still angry at me for cheating on him with Danny."

"The guy you used to work for?"

I nodded. "It was a mistake, but hell, you know these bikers," I said, lowering my voice. "I mean, it's okay for them to have sex with other women *anytime* they want. But God forbid if one of us reciprocates. They're a bunch of Neanderthals, if you ask me."

"I hear you," said Misty, chuckling. "Sometimes I wonder if they have more respect for their bikes than they do us."

"Oh, they definitely do. So, are you dating any of them?" I asked.

"Not really. I mean, I've had sex with a couple of the guys, for shits and giggles, you know? But, I'm not really seeing any of them seriously."

"Did you ever have sex with Tank?"

"Hell yeah. Not Raptor, though. Just so you know."

I chuckled. "I didn't think so but even if you did, I'm not worried about it," I replied, although, truthfully, I would have been really pissed.

"He must have really flipped out when you cheated on him. I can only imagine how that went, especially after his little tizzy here."

"He went ape-shit. Kicked me out of the house. I had to move in with Danny for a while, but now I'm back home with him. Where I should be. Things are going to work out, too."

"Really? Aren't you worried about him and Adriana?"

"He's just using her to get back at me," I said confidently. "Once our baby is born –"

Misty sucked in her breath. "Baby? What baby?"

I covered my mouth and laughed. "Oops. I'm not supposed to say anything. I'm pregnant."

"Trevor's?"

I nodded.

"And he knows about it?"

"That's why he let me move back in. Well, that and the fact that deep down, I know he still really loves me."

"Wow. That's just crazy."

"Crazy is right. Crazy love," I answered, sighing. "I just wish he'd forget about that bitch, Adriana, and realize that we're meant to be together."

"From the way he was talking earlier, he might not have a choice but to say 'baa-bye'," said Misty, waving her hand.

I giggled. "Exactly."

The front door opened and Slammer walked into the bar.

Misty straightened up. "Wonder what's up with him," she mumbled, noticing his stony expression.

"He always looks like he's pissed off about something," I whispered as he approached the bar. When our eyes met, I smiled at him. "Hi, Slammer."

He smiled, but it didn't reach his eyes. "How's it going, ladies? You keeping my customers happy?"

"Not as happy as the strippers," said Misty, nodding toward the stage where one of them was pretending to ride a bull, naked but wearing tassels.

Slammer turned to look at the stripper. "Nadine's got a new act, huh? Where'd they get the mechanical bull?"

"Not sure. It doesn't work, though. She just uses it as a prop," replied Misty.

He nodded and then looked at me. "How's it going? Catching onto things here?"

"Yes. Thanks so much for giving me a job. I don't know what I'd have done without you giving me this chance. Trevor –"

"Raptor, you mean," said Slammer, grabbing a toothpick. He stuck it between his teeth. "Use their Road Names in here."

"Oh, sure. Anyway, I'm just so grateful that you gave me a job." I leaned forward and lowered my voice. "I just wish I could repay you properly."

"What do you mean?" he asked, as Misty rushed over to the other side of the bar to refill a couple of beers.

I threw my hair over my shoulder and smiled. "Don't act like you don't know what I'm talking about," I whispered, staring up at him through my lashes. The truth was that I'd always secretly fantasized about giving the Gold Viper's president, Slammer oral. The thought of watching him lose control for a few seconds and to know that I was responsible for it was a real turn on.

"Darlin', if I wasn't happily engaged I might have taken you up on that offer," he replied, chuckling. "But, you know how it is."

"Too bad. If you ever change your mind…"

"What about Raptor?"

I let out a ragged sigh and stood up straighter. "He doesn't know what he wants."

"Bullshit. Raptor is one man who knows exactly what he wants," said Slammer.

Before I could respond, Misty walked back over to us. "You were gone most of the day," she said, filling a glass with tap beer. "Wasn't sure if you were coming in."

He cleared his throat. "Had some stuff to do. Where's Tank? In my office?"

Misty nodded. "I think so."

"Good. I have some news he's going to like. Something that's going to make all of us a shitload of money."

Her eyes widened. "Really? Does that mean I'll get a raise?"

"Oh, you'll get something out of the deal. Believe me," he told her, smiling. "I guarantee it."

I **WORKED UNTIL** seven and then left Griffin's. On my way home, I stopped at the grocery store and picked up the fixings for one of Trevor's favorite meals – lasagna. After the episode earlier, I doubted he would be bringing anyone home and wanted to do something special for him. After I finished buying the groceries, I stopped by a liquor store and picked up a bottle of tequila, another of his vices. I decided that if I offered him comfort food, a bottle to cry into, and a willing sex partner, he might realize that he didn't need Adriana after all. Not when he had me.

Looking forward to the night ahead, I pulled into Trevor's driveway and shut off the car. As I got out and walked back to the trunk to collect the groceries, I began to hum to myself. Grabbing the bag of food, I headed toward the porch and as I climbed the steps, a van pulled up into the driveway. Turning around, I realized that I didn't recognize the brown vehicle, but wasn't concerned. Trevor had a lot of friends and I could see that the two men in the front seat were both smiling, like we'd met before.

They got out of the van and approached me.

"Can I help you?" I asked, liking the way the taller one with the goatee and the multiple piercings had been checking me out. I'd promised myself that I would try and remain faithful from now on, but that didn't mean I couldn't enjoy other men's stares.

"Are you Raptor's Old Lady?" asked the guy with the piercings.

Raptor's Old Lady. I liked the sound of it. Always had. "Yeah," I replied, figuring that it would be my title again soon anyway. "I am."

The two strangers looked at each other and smiled.

91

FIFTEEN

ADRIANA

I'D BEEN DOING my homework at the public library, when my mother called me. It had been hard to concentrate, with the emotions rolling through me, but I'd persevered by reminding myself that I wasn't about to fail because of Trevor. If anything, my determination to graduate and get the hell out of Jensen was even stronger.

"You haven't been answering your calls," she scolded.

"Sorry, I'm in the library. I turned my phone down so I wouldn't disturb anyone with calls."

"The library? Why there? You never study at the library."

She was right but I didn't feel like explaining what had happened between me and Trevor and the chances of him hitting a library were pretty slim. "I needed some books," I lied.

"Oh. Well, Trevor was just here, looking for you."

Rolling my eyes, I uncapped the bottle of water I'd been drinking. "Oh, yeah?" I said, taking a sip. "He actually showed up at the store?"

"Yes. He's been trying to call you, too. Are you avoiding him?"

I sighed. She was so nosy and persistent. I just didn't have the strength to talk about it, nor did I want to start crying in the library. Just thinking about the phone call from earlier made my heart ache. "I really don't want to talk about it now, Mom."

"Hmm... You *are* avoiding him."

"Maybe, but I really don't want to discuss this right now, okay?" I said, lowering my voice when I noticed one of the librarians raising her eyebrows at me.

"He's going back to the house to see if you're home."

"Obviously, I'm not."

"Obviously. Did you two get into a fight?"

"Like I said, I really don't want to talk about it and I have to go, anyway," I whispered, catching the librarian's eye again. I smiled weakly at her. Fortunately, she smiled back and went back to whatever she was typing on at her desk. "I have all of this studying to do, you know?"

"I understand. Are you still nauseous?"

"No."

"Good. I'll call Trevor and let him know that you're fine but that he still needs to leave you alone because you're studying."

My eyes widened in horror. "*What*? No, Mom. I don't need your help with him, okay? And how did you get his phone number anyway?"

"I copied it from your cell phone," she said. "You know, in case of emergencies. I need to know how to get ahold of you."

I let out a ragged sigh. "Right. Just... don't start calling him, okay? For God's sake, I'm twenty-one years old. I don't need your help with something like this."

"Something like what?"

I rolled my eyes in exasperation. "Men."

"I'm just trying to help, you know."

"Then help me by minding your own business," I said firmly, although regretting the words immediately. Vanda was so sensitive and I could imagine the hurtful expression on her face.

"Fine," she answered, her voice brittle. "But, when you're a parent, you'll understand. I only want what's best for you."

"I know and I really do appreciate your concern," I whispered, noticing the librarian staring at me again. "But I'm a big girl, Mom. You keep forgetting that." Like, every day.

"I know." She sucked in her breath. "Oh, I have to go. Two of my best clients just walked in the front door. Mr. and Mrs. Parker. You remember them, don't you?"

"Yes."

"Mr. Parker called earlier and said it was their anniversary. They're picking out jewelry together, again."

The wealthy couple owned three restaurants in Iowa and usually spent a fortune on jewelry when they visited. Oddly enough, Mrs. Parker was very fussy and always picked out what her husband gave her. There were obviously no surprises in that relationship. I almost envied them at the moment.

"Well, good luck. Sell them on everything."

Vanda laughed. "I'll try," she said before hanging up.

As I was about to put my cell phone back into my purse, I noticed that Trevor had left yet another message and sighed.

A FEW HOURS later, I began packing up my homework. It was after seven, I was hungry, tired, and wanted nothing more than to crawl into my bed and sleep for the next couple of days. But, still leery of Trevor waiting for me on my doorstep, I decided to make a detour to a local coffee shop just up the road from my house. When I arrived, I went inside and ordered a strawberry-banana smoothie and a turkey club sandwich on honey-wheat bread. Then, I slipped into a back booth and hung out there for a while, taking small bites of my food as I played games on my cell phone. After I finished eating, I emptied the tray and headed home, realizing that I couldn't stay away forever. I decided that if Trevor did have the audacity to show up, I'd tell him where to go with his apologies. There wasn't anything that he could say that would excuse his cheating and I wasn't the naïve little suburban girl he may have thought I was.

It was five-minutes-to-nine when I finally pulled into my garage and shut the engine off. Grabbing my backpack, I got out, locked the car, and was about to shut the garage door, when I noticed a tall shadow moving near the edge of the driveway. Thinking that it was Trevor, I quickly pressed the garage door button to close it. Unfortunately, I was too late and a man ducked underneath the door, causing it to lift back up.

"Don't be frightened," said the stranger, holding up his hands. "I don't mean you any harm."

"Who are you? What do you want?" I asked, trying not to panic. He was tall, had long hair, a shitload of piercings, and wore a black leather jacket. When I noticed the biker patches, I could barely breathe. I'd seen them before; he was a Devil's Ranger.

Noticing my terror, his eyes glinted in the darkness. "Relax, darlin'. Name's Skull. I'm looking for Raptor. Is he here?"

"No," I replied, looking around for something to protect myself. The Devil's Rangers had killed my best friend and now one of them was standing in my garage. In didn't take rocket science to figure out that I was in deep shit.

"Do you know where I can find him?"

I prayed that he was only there for Trevor and that he'd leave me alone, especially when he found out that I had no idea where Trevor was. "I don't know where he is."

Skull smiled. "You're Adriana, aren't you?"

I just stared at him.

Still Smiling, he took another step toward me. "Yeah, you are. I have the right girl."

Sirens were blaring in my head but I was frozen with fear. I needed to do something, but I just couldn't move. "What do you mean?"

He quickly reached into his pocket and pulled out a gun. "We're going for a ride," he said, pointing it at me. "Scream, and I'll fucking shoot you."

Thinking that I was dead the moment I got into his vehicle anyway, I spun around and ran into my house.

"Bad move, you little bitch!" he called as I slammed the door.

Crying, I bolted it and ran toward the kitchen, meaning to escape through the sliding glass door. As I reached it, however, I found another biker staring at me from the other side of the glass. He smiled triumphantly and waved a switchblade. Gasping in fear, I turned and ran toward the other end of the house just as Skull kicked the garage door open.

"Quit fucking around!" he hollered.

Remembering how they'd savagely murdered Krystal, I ignored him and ran to the front door.

"Stop right there!" ordered Skull, somewhere behind me.

Trembling so violently that I could barely get the door unlocked, I threw it open and ran across the lawn. "Help me!" I screamed, trying to get one of the neighbors' attention. Nobody was outside but most of the people living on our block were retired and usually attune to what was going on in the neighborhood. In other words, they were nosy. Normally this bugged the hell out of me but at that moment, I could only hope that someone was peeking out of their windows.

When I reached the curb, a dark brown van came out of nowhere, arriving at a screaming halt. As I tried to run the other way, another Devil's Ranger leaped out of the vehicle and caught me. He grabbed me around the waist as and clamped a hand over my mouth, cutting off my screams.

"Leave her alone!" hollered a man across the street. It sounded like Mr. Barnes, who always brought my mother tomatoes from his garden and snow-blowed our driveway. "I'll call the cops!"

"Fuck off!" yelled one of the bikers. "Or I'll put a bullet in your head, old man!"

I couldn't hear his response because I was thrown into the van.

"No!" I screamed, crawling back to the door, as they slammed it shut. Sobbing, I began pounding on it with my fists. "Help me!"

The van started moving and I was thrown backward, into a woman I hadn't noticed before. She was curled up in a fetal position and appeared to be in pain.

"Oh, my God, I'm sorry. Are you okay?" I asked, feeling an odd sense of relief that I wasn't alone. But then, when she raised her head, I noticed that someone had used her face as a punching bag.

"Okay? Does it look like I'm okay?" she mumbled, opening one black eye.

Recognizing the blonde hair and familiar voice, I stared at the other woman in horror. "Brandy?"

SIXTEEN

RAPTOR

FRUSTRATED AND TIRED of driving, I went back to Griffin's. When I arrived, Slammer and Tank were sitting outside in the darkness, their backs against the picnic table. They were both having a smoke and talking quietly; I could see from the lines on Slammer's face that he was exhausted.

"Did Chopper find anything?" I asked, shoving my keys into my leather.

"No. Doesn't look like we've been wired or bugged," he replied. His legs were stretched out and he was staring down at his black leather boots, which appeared to be brand new. "Like 'em?" he asked, noticing me looking.

I nodded. "Yeah. They new?"

"Yep. Frannie got them for me today at the mall. She's a good woman. Always doing stuff. Frets over me like I'm one of her kids." He let out a ragged sigh.

"What's wrong?" asked Tank.

Slammer smashed the end of his cigarette on the picnic table and stood up. "I don't know. Maybe I'm thinking that we should wait on the wedding. With all this shit that's going on with Mud, it could get uglier before it gets better."

"Thought you had a plan," I replied.

"I do, but they don't always fucking work the way you want them to, do they?" he snapped.

Tank and I looked at each other.

Slammer rubbed the side of his face and looked at me again. "Sorry. I'm just stressed out. Shouldn't be taking it out on you."

"I'm not complaining," I said, knowing I was just as guilty at times.

"Listen, Pop, don't let this shit with Mud interfere with the wedding," said Tank.

"I'm more worried about Frannie's welfare than the wedding itself," he said.

"You think Mud will come after her?" I asked.

"He might try. Look at what he did to Krystal. I can't watch her twenty-four hours a day, either. Even if I wanted to, she wouldn't let me."

"We need to get things rolling and do something before they come after us," said Tank."

"He's right," I said, reluctantly. "Something needs to be done, *now*."

"See," said Tank. "Even Raptor agrees. Fuck setting Mud up. Fuck sending him to prison. He doesn't deserve three hots and a cot. He deserves three shots and a hole in the ground."

"It's not that easy. We kill him and one of us is going to prison," said Slammer.

"We won't get caught. We'll get an alibi."

"It's a nice assumption but I'm not willing to risk the chance. Too many people watching us now as it is." He looked at his watch. "It's getting late. Let's go inside and I'll make a few phone calls. I'd like to see if we can set Mud up to take a fall."

"Make sure it's one that he can't get up from," mumbled Tank.

"That's the idea," he replied.

We followed Slammer to the entrance, all of us quiet. I knew exactly where Slammer was coming from – Mud dies and we'd be the first suspects. The heat was definitely watching us; I'd even seen some unmarked squads circling my block a few days back.

"If it doesn't work out, this plan of yours, why don't we just hire The Judge again?" asked Tank, when we were back inside of the bar.

"He's expensive," he replied. "Let me think about things some more. I'll see if we can find a way to take care of that prick ourselves," he said, raising his voice.

I could barely hear him. It was after nine and the place was now packed. Two strippers were on stage, straddling a motorcycle together, while the speakers pounded out an old song, "Girls, Girls, Girls," by Motley Crew.

"Whose Harley is that?" I asked, staring at the bike.

"It's Hilary's," said Tank, nodding toward the strippers. "She wanted to use it for her act."

"How'd you get it up there?" I asked.

"We used the ramp in back," he replied.

The red-head, who was also the owner of the bike, noticed us staring and blew a kiss our way.

"She looks a little like Adriana, doesn't she?" asked Tank.

"Fuck no. Adriana is gorgeous," I said.

"So is Hilary," replied Tank.

"You actually looked at her face?" joked Slammer.

Tank chuckled. "It wasn't easy."

As we made our way to the bar, my cell phone began to ring. I pulled it out of my jacket and looked at the caller ID. It wasn't a number I recognized.

"Hello?" I answered.

"Trevor? Is that you?"

"Yes it is," I replied, recognizing Vanda's voice.

"Oh, thank God!" she cried, hysterical. "We need your help!"

A cloud of doom filled the skies above me. "What's wrong?"

"It's Adriana… she's been kidnapped!"

SEVENTEEN

ADRIANA

"WHAT IN THE hell is going on?" I asked Brandy, trembling. "Do you know why they've taken us?"

She took a while to answer. "Isn't it obvious? Retaliation."

I brushed the tears from my cheeks and then tucked my knees against my chest. "Retaliation. Again. Does it ever end?" I mumbled, thinking about Krystal again.

"I guess it will when they're all dead," she replied, now trying to sit up. Her face contorted with pain and I watched as she wrapped her arms around her stomach. As angry as I was at Brandy for screwing Trevor, even I couldn't help but feel a twinge of sympathy for her. Someone had obviously beaten the hell out of the girl.

"Someone already has, but obviously it wasn't enough." I sighed. "They did this to you?"

Brandy nodded and touched her cheek. She winced. "I called one of them an asshole and I guess he just had to prove I was right."

"Did they hurt your stomach at all?" I asked, wondering about the baby.

She touched her belly. "They were pretty rough with me. I don't think they harmed anything. Although," she closed her eyes, "at this point, it probably doesn't even matter."

"Of course it matters," I said, shocked. For someone so determined to have Trevor, she was giving up so easily on her life and the life of her baby.

Brandy opened her eyes. "Why, do you think they'll let us go?" she said, laughing coldly.

"If they don't, we can always try and escape."

"I doubt we'll have the chance."

"You never know."

"No, I guess you don't."

We were silent for a while, staring at each other.

"Do you have any idea why they've taken *us*?" I replied, breaking the silence. "Besides the retaliation? Did they say anything?"

She shook her head. "All I know is that they were looking for Raptor's Old Lady."

"So they took *both* of us?"

"I guess they didn't want to get the wrong girl."

"I just don't get it. Why us in particular? They must really hate Trevor."

"You think?" she muttered, sarcastically.

"Maybe they want something from him. God, I hope he cooperates. If that's the case," I said, talking more to myself, "we might actually walk out of this mess alive."

"Not before the Devil's Rangers fuck with us first."

The thought of being raped or beaten frightened me even more. I almost preferred a quick death. We needed to find a way out of there. Both of us. I looked down at her belly. "Did you tell them you were pregnant?"

"I didn't have much time for chit chat," she said dryly.

"Maybe if you would have told them –"

"They don't fucking care," she snapped, looking at me like I was an idiot. "Look, you don't know how horrible these bastards are. The Devil's Rangers pride themselves on being as bad-assed as possible. It's their M.O. They certainly don't give a shit about anyone not associated with their club. Hell, from what I hear, they don't even treat their own Old Ladies very well."

I clenched my jaw. "Actually, I know more about what kind of pricks they are than you think. They killed my best friend."

She was silent for a few minutes. "That girl they killed, Krystal. She was your friend, wasn't she?"

I nodded.

She sighed. "I wonder if they'll take us all the way to their clubhouse. From what I've heard, they moved it Minnesota."

I was beginning to feel nauseous again. "I hope not, although, maybe it will give us more time to come up with an escape plan."

She snorted. "Give it up on the escape plan. We're both fucked."

I wanted to believe that she was being overly dramatic, but deep down, I had to agree.

EIGHTEEN

RAPTOR

"What do you mean she's been kidnapped?" I asked, Vanda, shocked.

Tank's head whipped around. "Who's been kidnapped?"

"Adriana," I mouthed.

He turned to Slammer, who looked just as stunned.

"The neighbors called and said that two men, driving in a brown van, snatched her from the yard," she said.

"Did they get a description of the men or a license plate?"

"Not too much, because it was dark. The neighbor across the street said that it was hoodlums with biker emblems like..." she stopped.

"Like me?" I said dryly.

"That's what I was told."

"Did they see the patches?" I asked, although it was pretty obvious. The Devil's Rangers had taken her. It was the only thing that made sense.

"I don't know. Look, I've got to go. I'm heading home to meet with the police. You should talk to them too. I know you know something about this, Trevor."

"I have no idea who kidnapped her, Vanda," I lied, not wanting to waste my time talking to the police. "I've got nothing for them."

"You're lying," she said angrily. "Don't do this. You need to talk to them. If anything happens to Adriana, I'll just die."

"I'll check around and see if I can find out who might have taken her," I replied, ignoring her comment. She was right, after all. "I won't stop until I find out who has her, and then I'll talk to the cops, if it helps us get her back."

She began to cry again. "Okay. Find my baby. Please, Trevor. I'd do anything to have her back."

I felt the same way.

NINETEEN

MUD

MUD WAS SITTING at his desk, getting a blow job, when his cell phone rang. He reached over and grabbed it. "Keep going," he said to the blonde, April, who was on her knees. "This shouldn't take long."

She smiled up at him.

"The shipment is on the way," said Skull.

"Good. Any problems?"

"Almost, but we handled it."

He sucked in his breath as the girl's head bobbed faster. "Explain," he said, sliding his hand into her mass of platinum blonde curls. One thing about April – she looked and sucked like a porno star.

"Let's just say that we have two. One who we picked up at his house and the other, we picked up at a different address."

"He has two?"

"Not really. It's complicated," answered Skull, sounding amused. "What's happening on your end of the phone, Mud? Sounds like I'm interrupting something."

"It's none of your goddamn business. Now, tell me we have what we need?"

"And then some."

"Good. See you soon," he answered and then hung up.

April raised her head. "I'm so horny, Mud. How about I get naked and you fuck me?" she asked, sliding her hand up and down his shaft.

"Another time." He pushed her head back down. He'd forgotten to pick up more condoms and the fuck if he was going to take a chance with April. Although a real looker, it was pretty obvious that she wanted to be more than a piece of tail. She wanted to wear his cut and ride on the back of his bike. But he didn't want an Old Lady, nor did he want to take a chance and knock her up. Eighteen years of child support was bullshit. He hated kids and he wasn't about to have one with a girl who whined as much as April. "Yeah, open wide," he ordered, thrusting his hips so she'd take it deeper into her mouth. He closed his eyes and thought about how pissed off Raptor was going to be when he realized what had happened. That he'd taken *his* precious Old Lady. He imagined the things that he'd do to her when she arrived, which would be anything the fuck he wanted. Hell, as far as he was concerned, the girl would be passed around and then disposed of.

She's property of the Devil's Rangers now.

Thoughts of fucking Raptor's bitch's mouth, instead of April's sent him over the edge. He gasped as his seed exploded out of his dick. "That's it, baby," he growled. "Swallow it." She obliged and when his penis became too sensitive, he pushed her away.

April tumbled backward on her heels. "Mud," she whined, staring up at him with swollen lips and big doe eyes. "What the hell?"

"Quit fucking around and get me some coffee," he ordered, pulling his Levis back up. The truth was, making her feel insignificant gave him a tiny thrill.

She scowled at him. "Really?"

Mud grunted. "Hey, you're the one who wanted to suck my dick when all I really wanted was a damn cup of coffee. Now, you can go and get what I asked for in the first place."

April stood up. She was wearing a skin-tight, blue dress and knee-high black boots. He'd once found her sexier than hell, but now all he could think about was her community snatch. In the last week-and-a-half, it had given more rides than any rollercoaster at Disney World, regardless of whether she'd wanted it or not. But it was a rule that any girl who hung out at the clubhouse was open season and the guys loved April more than any of the other whores that visited. He had a feeling that her black hole of a vagina could now take all of them at once, if ordered to, and Mud was secretly glad he'd forgotten to buy condoms. He didn't want to go in and end up in some other galaxy.

"Why do you have to be so mean?" she asked, still pouting.

He laughed coldly. "You've never seen my *mean* side, sweetheart. But if you don't quit acting like a fucking baby, you just might. Now," he rubbed his eye, "get me what I asked for and quit with the griping. You know how much I hate that shit."

April nodded quietly and then walked out of his office.

"Fucking bitches," he mumbled, taking out a cigarette. They always wanted or needed something. Just like his mother, who'd nagged him until the day she'd died. If it wasn't for the lung cancer taking her life, he'd have done it himself. He'd come close more than a few times.

April returned a few seconds later with his coffee, still looking pissed. Sighing, he opened up his desk drawer and took out a joint. He held it up to her. "Why don't you go find a quiet place and smoke this? It might make you less *uptight.*"

Her eyes widened in surprise and she smiled. "Thanks, Mud."

"Don't say I never gave you anything," he said as she leaned over the desk to give him a kiss. He held his arm out, to stop her. "No need for that. Not after you just swallowed my load."

She laughed and tucked the joint behind her ear. "Fine. You guys are all weird about that."

"If I wanted to taste another man's wad, I'd become a faggot."

Her eyes narrowed. "My brother is gay. He hates that word. So do I. It's offensive and hateful."

"Oh really? Well, tough shit. You're in my clubhouse and I'll say whatever the fuck I want," he said, raising his voice. "You don't like it then you can give me back my joint and go home to your asshole faggot of a brother and fuck him straight. You've had enough practice in that department. If anyone can do it, you certainly can."

Tears sprang to her eyes and she clenched her fists together. Nobody was as cruel as Mud. Nobody. "You're... you're..."

"I'm what?" he asked, daring her to say it. He knew he was being an asshole but didn't give a shit.

The look in Mud's eyes reminded her of the time he'd beat one of the other girls so badly, she'd ended up in the hospital. April decided to let it go. She'd had enough of his bullshit but she wasn't about to get a beating from a prick that enjoyed using his fists on women. Not when there were other ways of getting back at him, which she vowed to. "You're... so generous," she lied, wishing that she could slap the slimy smile right off of his face. "For giving me this joint."

His eyes widened and he laughed. "Good choice of words. Not even I was expecting that. Now, get the fuck out of my office. I've got some calls to make."

She turned on her heel and left, her nails digging into the palms of her hands.

I hope someone takes you down, you prick, thought April, wishing she would have bit his dick off when she had the chance.

TWENTY

RAPTOR

"WHAT'S THIS ABOUT Adriana?" asked Slammer after I hung up with Vanda.

"They've got her," I said angrily. My hands were shaking, I was so pissed off. "Where's Misty?"

"I think she left," said Tank, scratching the stubble on his chin.

"She did," said Slammer, pulling out his cell phone. "I'm calling this in. Let everyone know what's going on. Fuck, I might even call Bastard on this one."

Trying not to lose it, I headed toward the exit. I was furious but I was also terrified. For Adriana. If they were the ones that had grabbed her, she might already be dead.

"Where you going?" asked Tank, following me.

"I'm going to Misty's and then to Minnesota if I have to," I said, my voice cracking. "I've gotta find her, brother."

"I'm coming with you," he said, when we stepped back outside into the cold. "You packing?"

I turned back around. "No, but I sure as shit need to be."

"Don't worry about driving home for it. I've got something in the safe for the both of us. Hang tight," he said, turning back around.

I waited for him in my truck. When he stepped back out of the bar, Slammer was with him.

"He's coming with us," said Tank, handing me a revolver.

I put the gun in the glove compartment. "Okay. We're going to Misty's place, right?"

"Yeah. I'll follow you in my vehicle," said Slammer, nodding toward his black Yukon Denali.

Tank got into my truck and started making phone calls to other club members, telling them to stand by for instructions.

"You think Misty knows about this?" he asked between calls.

"I don't know but I'm going to fucking kill her," I said, gritting my teeth, "if she doesn't help us find Adriana."

"She will when we get our hands on her. We'll make her tell us everything, even if we have to beat it out of her," he replied. "You know where she lives?"

"Kind of. She lives in that trailer park near St. Peter's, doesn't she?" I answered.

"Yeah. You know which trailer?"

"No."

"I'll direct you."

"Okay."

When we arrived at Misty's, her car was parked in the small driveway and the light was on.

Slammer pulled in behind me and we all got out.

"I thought that was you. What are you guys doing here?" asked Misty, opening the front door before we had a chance to knock. She blew out a cloud of smoke and smiled. "Are you looking to party?"

"Fuck no. We're here to talk," I said sharply, trying to keep my cool.

"Talk? *Now*?" she asked, looking surprised. She moved out of the way so that we could enter. "This couldn't wait until tomorrow?"

We stepped into the trailer; it smelled like the fruity perfume she always wore and stale cigarettes.

"Seriously," she went on. "What's so important that the three of you had to drive all the way out here when you could have just called me?"

"Quit with the bullshit," I said, turning around to face her, my heart pounding in my chest. I felt like grabbing the two-faced, conniving bitch and throwing her across the room. "Where the fuck is Adriana?"

"Your Old Lady?" Misty's eyes widened. "Why would I know where *she* is?"

Slammer sighed and pulled out a gun. "Enough with the lies, Misty. Tell us where she is or I'll blow your fucking head off. We have no time for this shit. A girl's life is in danger."

She took a step back. "Why are you telling me all of this stuff?" she asked, looking frightened. "I have no idea what you're even talking about."

"We know all about you and your dealings with the Devil's Rangers," snapped Tank.

"The Devil's Rangers?" she laughed nervously. "What the fuck, Tank? Why would I have any dealings with them?"

"That's the question, isn't it?" said Slammer, grabbing her by the arm. He held the gun to her forehead. "Why would you fuck us over for those pieces of shit?"

She began to cry. "Please, don't kill me. I don't know anything about Adriana. I swear to God."

"Liar," I said, feeling so frustrated, I wanted to grab her and shake the truth from her. "They have her and you know it. Where in the fuck have they taken her?"

She shook her head quickly. "I don't know. I don't. Please, you've got to believe me."

Her cell phone, which was sitting on the coffee table in front of the sofa, began to vibrate. Tank leaned over and picked it up. "Looks like you have a text message, Misty," he said, pushing some buttons. "From someone named 'M'. Who's 'M'?"

"My mom," she said quickly. She held out her hand. "She's very sick. I need to read the message."

Tank grunted. "Don't worry, I'll read it to you."

"Please, just give me my phone," she begged, her lips trembling.

"It says that you need to get out of town, Misty." Tank looked at her and smirked. "What do you think that means?"

"That she needs me," she said.

"Still playing games, huh? Do you really think we're that stupid?" replied Tank. He typed something into her phone and sent it.

"What did you type?"

"I asked 'M' why," he said.

"You're looking a little warm, there, Misty," said Slammer, staring at the beads of sweat on her forehead.

"You'd be sweating too if you had a gun pointed at your head," she snapped.

The phone vibrated again. Tank read the message quietly and then looked at me.

"What does it say?" I asked.

"It says that they have something of Raptor's and that he'll be looking for it," he replied, smiling grimly.

"Busted, you fucking bitch," said Slammer.

She looked at me. "I swear to God, I had no idea that they were going to do something this."

"Enough with the lies!" I hollered, staring at her in disbelief.

"Your words don't mean shit to us right now," said Slammer in a deadly voice.

Tank typed something else and sent it.

"What did you type?" I asked, pacing back and forth in the trailer.

"I asked what exactly that meant."

After a few seconds, the phone buzzed again.

"It says not to worry about it and that she needs to get to Minnesota," read Tank...

"This is bullshit. Give me the phone. I'm calling him," said Slammer.

"You think that's a good idea?" asked Tank.

"You gotta better one? Adriana's life is on the line. We need to try and resolve this without her getting hurt," said Slammer.

Sighing, Tank handed the phone to him.

Slammer shoved Misty toward me.

"I'm so sorry," she wept. "I didn't think they were going to kidnap your girl."

"What the fuck did you think they were going to do?" I snapped at her.

"I don't know. I –"

"Shut up, Misty," warned Slammer, putting the phone on "speaker."

"Yeah?" said the voice. It was definitely Mud's.

"It's Slammer."

There was a long pause. "Slammer, huh? What's up?"

Slammer laughed coldly. "What's up? You know exactly what's up. Where have you taken Adriana?"

"Adriana? Adriana who?" he replied, sounding bored.

I grit my teeth. "You know exactly who, motherfucker."

Mud chuckled. "That you, Raptor? How are things going these days?"

"Listen to me," I growled, "you fucking piece of shit. You'd better let her go or I'll –"

"You'll *what*?" he hollered. "Send The *Judge* to come looking for me? Your crazy, psychotic brother?"

Slammer and I looked at each other.

"Didn't think I knew, did you?" asked Mud.

"What the fuck do you want?" asked Slammer.

"I think you already know the answer to that."

"Cut the bullshit," said Slammer. "What the hell do you want because we really don't fucking know."

He sighed. "At first, I just wanted straight revenge, for all of the shit you've caused for us. Burning down our building, threatening us with some bullshit story about having proof that we were somehow involved in Krystal's death. I mean, where did you come up with that? Shit, Tank probably killed her when he was fucking that little bitch."

"You piece of shit!" snarled Tank. "You're fucking done, man. Done!"

"Watch your mouth, *Son!*" shouted Mud. "Right now, I've got the floor and I've got the goods, so you listen up and keep your shit quiet!"

"What do you want?" asked Slammer before Tank could respond.

"I've been thinking," he replied, in a friendlier voice. "There have been enough deaths, don't you think?"

"There certainly has and that girl you've got, Adriana? You need to let her go. If you don't, the war we've shared in the past will look like a fucking cookie convention," warned Slammer. "I'm as serious as shit about it, too. Let her go."

"Actually, I have two girls who should be arriving here shortly. Adriana and some girl named, Brandy. If I remember correctly, you two were an item once, weren't you, Raptor?"

My eyes widened in surprise. "You have Brandy, too?"

"It was an accident. She claimed to be your Old Lady when we picked her up outside your house. Fortunately, she confessed to who your *real* Old lady was and now we have both."

"Are either of them hurt?" asked Slammer.

"They're alive. That's all you need to know."

"Listen to me, Mud, Brandy is pregnant," said Slammer, looking at me. "If someone beat her, she might need to see a doctor."

Mud laughed. "Pregnant, huh? Tough break. Is that your brat, Raptor?"

"Fuck off," I muttered.

He laughed.

"Enough of the bullshit. What do you want from us?" asked Slammer.

"I want two-hundred-fifty grand to start out with. I also want The Judge. Give me those two things and I'll give you what you want."

I swore. Two-hundred-fifty thousand dollars. I didn't have that kind of money. My house wasn't even worth that much.

"Why do you want The Judge?" asked Slammer.

"He killed Breaker. Why do you think?"

"Are you trying to tell me that all of this is because of that shit-bag, Breaker?" sneered Slammer, staring at us in disbelief.

"He was a Devil's Ranger. You can't tell me you wouldn't want to avenge the death of one of your brothers," he answered.

"I wouldn't have a piece of shit in my club and I certainly

wouldn't consider him a brother," replied Slammer.

"Bullshit, you have several degenerates in your club. What the fuck are you talking about?" said Mud.

"What a crock of shit," I said. "We don't rape innocent women. We don't have to."

"You lying cocksucker," he said, laughing. "You all act like you're a bunch of choir boys but you don't fool me. Besides, Misty tells a different tale."

We all looked at her and she shook her head quickly.

"Speaking of Misty, we have her in our custody, obviously," said Tank. "You interested in a trade?"

Mud laughed. "Why the fuck would I want Misty? She's of no use to me. Not now, anyway."

Misty's mouth dropped. "Excuse me?"

"Oh, there she is. Enjoying the conversation, darlin'?"

"Fuck you, Mud," she snapped.

"Done that and you're still not worth the trade. No offense."

Her eyes filled with tears. "You... you fucking lied to me. You said that you'd always take care of me."

"That was Breaker. I don't recall saying anything to you other than 'bend over so I can do you doggy-style'." He howled in laughter at his own joke.

"You're such an asshole!" she cried, staring at us in shame.

"Jesus, will someone just keep her fucking quiet, she's giving me a headache," said Mud, no longer laughing.

She was about to tell him off again when Tank pointed at her and mouthed "Don't."

Misty's eyes hardened.

"So let me get this straight," said Slammer. "We give you two-hundred-and-fifty grand, and you'll let those girls go?"

"The money along with The Judge," he replied. "I'll let you have them."

"I don't think he's going to be a willing participant," said Slammer.

"That's your problem. I'll give you until midnight tomorrow. I want the money in unmarked bills, by the way, and that asshole delivered to me, or the deal is off."

"Where do we make this *deal*?" asked Slammer, as if it was achievable

"Don't worry about the location right now. Set it up and call me back when you have the other details figured out."

"I don't know. We're going to need more time than that," said Slammer.

"Take it or leave it," he replied

Slammer looked at me. "We'll take it."

"I thought so," he replied and then hung up.

"You're really going to pay that asshole?" asked Tank.

"Fuck no," he replied, smiling. "One thing about Mud is that he never thinks these things through."

"What about Adriana?" I asked, frustrated. "I need to get her back."

"Don't worry about it, Raptor. You will," said Slammer, pulling out his phone. "In fact, I'm going to track The Judge down right now."

"In other words, you're paying Jordan and not Mud," I replied, relaxing slightly.

"Of course. He wants The Judge, that's the one thing we're going to make sure he gets. I think The Judge will be interested in Mud's obsession with him, too. Hell, maybe he'll even kill the sonofabitch for nothing."

"If he agrees to help us, I want to be there when it happens. I want to make sure Adriana isn't hurt when the shit goes down," I said.

"Same here," said Tank. "I want to see that fucker pay." He looked at Misty, who was listening in. "What do we do about her?"

"Hey, I'm innocent in all of this," she said quickly. "I mean, at least this thing with Adriana."

"Shut the fuck up, Misty," I said, my patience for her long gone.

"I just can't believe you did all of this because of Breaker," said Tank, staring at her in disgust. "A convicted rapist. What kind of demented human being are you?"

"You can't help who you love and... I swear to God, I didn't tell Mud anything about Adriana or Brandy," she said, crying again. "He wanted to know about your club's business affairs. I didn't even know much about that. I barely gave him any information. I swear to you..."

Slammer laughed coldly. "That's all, huh? You've been spying on us since the day I hired you! Feeding them information. You're lucky we don't put a bullet in your head."

Her eyes widened. "No, I wasn't spying on you back then. I met Breaker *after* you hired me."

"It doesn't matter one way or another," he replied. "You've fucked us over and now you're going to help us fuck Mud over. You feel me?"

She nodded quickly. "Yes. Whatever you want. I'll do it."

"Damn right you will," I said angrily. "And if Adriana dies, you're as good as dead yourself."

TWENTY ONE

ADRIANA

ENTALLY EXHAUSTED FROM everything that had happened to me that day, I fell asleep in the van. A couple of hours later, I woke to the sound of the door being opened. My back was stiff and sore from lying on the hard floor, but I moved away from the back door quickly, frightened of what they were planning to do with us.

"Wakey, wakey," said Skull, smiling coldly in the moonlight. "Your limo ride has come to an end, I'm afraid."

"Fuck you," mumbled Brandy.

"Let's wait and get you cleaned up first," he said, winking at her. "Then we'll talk about it."

"I'd rather die than let you touch me," she said, glaring at him.

"That can also be arranged." He pulled out a gun and pointed it at us. "Get out. Now."

We obeyed, although Brandy moved very slowly, which irritated Skull.

"Come on, we don't have all day," he muttered, waving the gun. "Get that ass moving, bitch."

"She's hurt," I said, sliding out of the van. I looked up at him. "Someone obviously beat the hell out of her."

"She's fine. Just a few bruises," he answered, peering at her face in the darkness. "Maybe now the cunt will follow orders without any lip."

"Cunt?" Brandy got out of the van and I watched in horror as she spit in his face.

"You fucking bitch!" he hollered and backhanded her.

Stumbling backwards, she put her hands to her face and began to cry.

I rushed to her side and touched her arm. "You okay?"

"Don't touch me," she hissed, jerking away from me.

"I'm just trying to help."

"I don't need it," she replied, looking away.

"God, I should just shoot you now," snapped Skull, wiping his face off. "We don't really need you anyway."

Just then, two other men rushed around the van, both of them pointing their guns at us.

"What's the problem?" asked one of them.

"That bitch spit in my face," said Skull, motioning toward Brandy.

"Yeah, but look at what you did to hers!" I cried surprising myself. "You beat the shit out of her and you're whining because she spit on your face?"

He took a step toward me and the look on his face chilled me to the bone. "Don't start with me, bitch. You'll be next. I don't give a fuck who you are, either."

Knowing what he was capable of, I held my tongue and looked away.

"Now, enough with the bullshit and get walking. Both of you," said Skull, motioning toward a shoddy two-story building with a red door and a sign that read "No Trespassing."

"Looks like Mud's the only one here," murmured one of the bikers as we walked past an old white pickup that was parked near the dumpsters. The garbage inside was bad enough to make me gag.

"Smells like death in there, doesn't it?" said Skull, noticing my sour expression. "You piss me off anymore and I'll put you in there with the trash. Of course, the smell won't bother you, because by then you'll be dead."

I ignored him.

When we got inside, the lights were on and I noticed that the place was similar to Griffin's, only without a stage. Besides there being a bar, there were two stripper poles, three pinball machines, and two pools table in the back next to an old jukebox.

"It's about time you made it," said a gravelly voice.

I turned toward a man getting up from a black leather sofa that was stationed near the back. He was naked from the waist up, muscular, and had several tattoos on his chest and arms. He looked like he was in his forties and reminded me a little of the actor, Danny Bonaduce, with his red hair and ruddy complexion.

He didn't say anything when he saw Brandy's swollen face, but his eyes widened in surprise when he noticed me. "Look at what we have here. You are not at all what I expected. I take it this is Adriana?" he said, turning to Skull. "Raptor's 'real' Old Lady?"

"I am not Raptor's 'real' Old Lady," I muttered.

His head snapped back toward me. "Is this the right girl, Skull?"

"It is, Mud," he answered, smirking. "She's lying."

So, this was Mud. "I'm *not* lying," I snapped, angrily. "I'm not with him. I'm not even dating him. As far as I'm concerned, Brandy is his Old Lady."

He looked at Brandy. "You're Raptor's Old Lady?"

She laughed coldly. "I don't know. He hasn't decided yet."

"You the pregnant one?" he asked her.

She nodded.

"They got you pretty good," he said, staring at her face. His eyes lowered. "You bleeding between your legs?"

"No," she answered quietly, looking embarrassed.

"Then you're probably fine."

"How do you know, are you a doctor?" she asked.

"No, but I'm the guy who says whether or not you're going to get another beating, so show some respect," he snapped.

She gritted her teeth together but didn't reply.

Grunting, he turned back to me. "What are you, a college student?"

I nodded.

His eyes traveled down my body. "I can see why Breaker was obsessed with a chick like you. You're definitely his type."

"What type is that?" I asked, scowling.

"Young and sweet," replied Mud, walking over to me. Before I could do anything, he grabbed me by the jaw and held it tightly while he examined my face like I was some kind of animal. "Skull, she looks like that actress, what's her name?" he asked, releasing me. "From Desperate Housewives. Eva something? She played Gabrielle."

"I don't know," said Skull. "Never watched it."

"Longoria," said one of the other men.

"That's right. I didn't care too much for the show but those bitches were hot. Especially her." He walked over to the bar and grabbed the bottle of whiskey that was sitting there. He unscrewed the cap and turned to me. "So, how desperate are you?" he asked, smiling darkly.

I didn't reply.

He took a swig of the bottle and then wiped his mouth. "Come on, now. What are you willing to do to walk out of here alive?"

"You'll let us walk out of here alive?" I asked.

"Maybe. See, I'm not the bad guy here. I've been forced into this situation by those bastards, the Gold Vipers."

My eyes narrowed. "Did they force you to kill Krystal?"

"Krystal? Oh, you're talking about the blonde, aren't you?" he said. "She was a little firecracker, that one. In a way, they did force me to kill her. Those assholes killed a part of my family and someone had to pay."

"She had nothing to do with the Gold Vipers," I said sharply. "Nothing."

"Wasn't she Tank's Old Lady?" he asked Skull.

He nodded.

"Well, there you go."

"No, they were only dating," I spat. "She was going to break up with him."

He snickered. "Oh. Well, I guess I saved her the aggravation."

I gritted my teeth. "You're a fucking jerk."

Instead of getting angry, he smiled. "A fucking jerk? No, what I am is a mother-fucking asshole. Your worst nightmare, if I want to be."

I opened up my mouth to respond when he pointed at me, his smile now gone.

"Know when to shut the fuck up and you might live longer."

I shut my mouth.

"Wise choice. See, I hold your life in my hands. I mean, you might be as sexy as fuck," he said, glancing down at my body again. "But, we will not tolerate any back talk from either of you. I think Brandy already learned her lesson."

I looked away.

"Speaking of Brandy, what should we do with her?" asked Skull.

"I don't know. Whatever the fuck you want. Just don't kill her," he replied.

Skull grabbed her by the arm. "I was hoping you'd say that. Let's go."

She tried pulling her arm away, but he grabbed her by the hair and started pushing her toward one of the hallways.

"Where are we going?" she cried, struggling.

He pulled her hair tighter. "You'll see when we get there."

"Please, let me go!" she sobbed.

"Shut up and walk!" he growled.

I took a step toward them. "Wait, please don't! You know she's pregnant. What kind of a monster are you?!"

He laughed. "Maybe if you're lucky, you'll get to find out later."

"Let her go!" I cried, moving toward them. I knew he was going to rape her and it tore me up inside.

One of the other bikers grabbed my arm and pulled me back.

Skull, looking frustrated, took his gun out of his jacket. He pointed it at her temple. "If you don't stop fucking around, I'll kill this bitch."

"He will, too, if you keep trying to interfere," said Mud calmly. I could tell by the look on his face that he was enjoying the scene.

"It's okay," said Brandy, forcing a smile through her tears. "I'll be fine."

I jerked my arm away from the guy holding me. "I doubt it. Not with that animal."

"Enough of the bullshit. Go easy on her," ordered Mud. He

turned and looked at me, a smirk on his face. "I don't want the bitch bleeding to death from a miscarriage. At least not until I get my money from Raptor. Then, as far as I'm concerned, both girls are free territory for anyone who wants a piece."

I stared at him in horror as I realized our situation was even worse than I'd thought. Even if Trevor gave him exactly what he wanted, Mud wasn't ever planning on letting us go.

TWENTY TWO

TWO

RAPTOR

AFTER SLAMMER LEFT a message for The Judge, we brought Misty back to the clubhouse with us to keep an eye on her. Fortunately, she gave us the directions to Mud's new setup in Minnesota without hesitation. I could tell that she was cooperating only because she was frightened of what we were going to do with her when it was all said and done.

"We should let the rest of our crew know what's going on," said Tank, rubbing his eye. It was just us three standing by the bar. Misty had fallen asleep on one of the sofas nearby and was snoring softly. "Maybe they can help."

"It's after midnight. Let them sleep. Not a whole lot they can do, unless they're willing to contribute financially," replied Slammer, looking wearier than ever. "Which I wouldn't expect them to do, anyway."

"About that, I'll pay you back. Every single cent of whatever The Judge charges you," I told him. I'd never felt so committed to Slammer and the rest of the Gold Vipers as I did at that moment. The fact that he was willing to front me that kind of money to save Adriana, a girl he didn't even really know, meant more than I could ever express.

"I know you will, Raptor," he said, patting me on the shoulder. He smiled grimly. "Truth is, I feel responsible for this mess. If I wouldn't have hired The Judge to kill Breaker, Adriana and Brandy would be at home sleeping right now. And, Krystal," he looked at Tank, his face full of regret. "She'd still be alive."

"None of this is your fault," said Tank, looking cross. "Don't go blaming yourself. You pulled that shit before on me and I already told you not to come down on yourself like that."

"Tank's right. Breaker started this war when he raped Jessica," I replied. "Unfortunately, some people got into the crossfire, but seriously, Prez, nobody blames you for this shit."

"Still, I should have taken better precautions or at the very least, handled it differently from the very beginning," he muttered as his phone started ringing. He took it out of his belt and checked the screen.

"Who is it?" I asked.

"The man who will hopefully make all of this go away," he said, before answering. "Hey, Judge."

IT DIDN'T TAKE much to convince my half-brother, Jordan Steele, A.K.A. The Judge, to help us with Mud, especially when he learned of his demands.

"How did he react when you told him Mud wanted his head on a platter?" asked Tank.

"He was pretty fucking amused," said Slammer, chuckling. "Fact is, I think he's going to really enjoy killing Mud. If I didn't hate the bastard so much, I'd probably feel sorry for the dumb fucker."

"So, what *is* the plan?" I asked, looking at the clock. The hours were ticking by and although I'd been trying to keep my composure, underneath I was a fucking wreck. All I kept thinking about was going after Adriana myself, but Slammer had axed that idea from the get-go. He wanted to talk to Jordan first and not just go after the Devil's Rangers, guns blazing.

"He said he'll meet you out there. Around Six a.m. He'll call you in a couple of hours to let you know where exactly he wants to meet up with you, though. You ever been to Hayward, Minnesota?"

"No. Never. So, he's okay with working as a team on this one?" I asked, a little surprised.

"A two-man team. He said he just wants you."

I nodded. "Okay. I'm leaving now then."

Tank scowled. "What the fuck? I'm not allowed to help?"

Slammer sighed. "I know. I know. He said the more people involved, the more shit that can go wrong. Remember, he's used to working alone. The only reason he's agreeing to let Raptor help is because of who they're holding as hostage."

"What if something goes wrong?" asked Tank. "I mean they've got at least a dozen guys out there who'd take a bullet for Mud."

"The Judge is more than capable of handling this situation," said Slammer. "It's why he charges so damn much. He always gets the job done. You've heard the stories."

"Yeah, but… I need to be there when this goes down. Not just because Raptor and I are tight, but because of Krystal. I want to see that douchebag go down," he replied angrily. "You of all people know that, Pop."

"I understand, but he made it pretty clear that he doesn't play well with others. I wish I could talk him into letting you go, but the man was insistent and I don't want to look a gift horse in the mouth."

Tank shook his head in exasperation and mumbled something.

Slammer patted him on the back. "It's going to get done. You're just not going to have to get your hands dirty on this one."

"I *want* my hands dirty," he said. "With blood from cracking

Mud's head open with my fists."

"I feel you, son. I really do."

"I'd better get on the road," I said, taking out my truck keys. "How much is he charging us, anyway?"

"Actually, we didn't get around that," Slammer replied and then smiled. "Hell, to be honest, I think he might be doing this as a courtesy. Usually, he asks for the money upfront. This time the issue didn't even come up."

"Maybe it's not about the money on this one," I replied, thinking that I wouldn't care if I was paid if the roles were reversed.

"You might have something there," agreed Slammer. "The Judge doesn't like anyone threatening him."

Tank grabbed his jacket and slipped it on.

"Where you going?" asked Slammer.

"I'm following them out there, in case they need backup. Now hold up," he said, when Slammer opened his mouth to protest. "I'll stay far enough behind that I won't get in the way, but close enough that if I'm needed, I can haul ass and get to where I need to be quickly."

"It's a good idea," I said, looking at Slammer. "You just never know."

"Fine," he said. "Just keep out of the way, if you're not needed. I mean it, Tank."

"Do I ever get in the way of shit?" he replied, looking a little peeved.

Both Slammer and I looked at each other.

Tank meant well, most of the time, but he was also bullish and stubborn. Usually, he followed his old man's orders, but if he didn't agree with them, shit usually didn't go well. I only hoped this wasn't one of those times.

TWENTY THREE

ADRIANA

T HE OTHER TWO guys from the van smoked a joint together and then left to go eat somewhere, leaving me alone with Mud. I wasn't sure if I should be relieved, or more frightened. He kept watching me in a way that made my skin crawl.

"You tired?" he asked, stepping behind the bar again.

Hoping he'd leave me alone, I nodded. The fact was that I was too terrified to think about sleep.

"So am I but sleep is not my friend today," he said, pulling out a small plastic bag of white powder. He smiled at me. "But this is. You want some?"

"No," I replied quickly.

"Do you even want to know what this shit is before you refuse to try it?"

I shook my head. "I'm not into drugs."

He shrugged. "Fine. More for me."

I glanced around the clubhouse while he set up his fix, trying to find something I could use as a weapon or for defense. As if he could read my mind, he pulled a gun out from under the bar and raised it in the air.

"By the way, don't get any fucking ideas," he said, rubbing his nose, which was red from snorting some of the powder.

I just looked away.

"Why don't you go and make yourself at home on the couch over there? Take a nap."

I stared at the sofa, knowing that there was no way that I'd be able to close my eyes with Mud eyeballing me the way he had been. Plus, I couldn't help but feel anxious about what was happening to Brandy. It was pretty horrifying to know that a woman was being raped in the next room and there was nothing that I could do about it. As much as I disliked Brandy, I knew that I needed to find a way to help her escape. I wondered if I could somehow get the gun from Mud.

"Go on. I won't bite," he said, sounding amused.

"But you certainly let Skull bite, don't you?" I said dryly.

He slid the gun into the back of his jeans. "Why not? He did well for me today. I owe him."

"You owe him the opportunity to rape someone?" I asked shrilly.

He leaned down and snorted more of the powder. Grunting in satisfaction, he raised his head and rubbed underneath his nose. "You're wasting your time trying to put some kind of guilt trip on me. I couldn't care less if he kills her, let alone rapes her. I hate anything that has to do with the Gold Vipers," he said. "Including their bitches. Old or new. Doesn't matter."

"Because of Breaker?" I replied, wrinkling my nose in disgust.

"Breaker? Fuck, yeah. His death tore me up. We were tight."

"So, this is really what this is all about? Avenging Breaker's death?" I asked, knowing we'd already been through this conversation. I wanted to keep him talking, however, so we didn't run out of things to say and he decided to put his hands on me.

"Actually, our clubs have always had our differences and have always butted heads. This time, they've caused a major shit-storm by taking out one of my closest brothers. I'm not resting until I've hit every last one of those fucking Gold Vipers."

"I don't know where you've gotten your information from, but

I'm not a part of their club. I never was."

"That's not what I've been told. In fact," he waved his finger, "I know for a fact that Raptor gave Breaker some shit for harassing a girl at Griffin's a few weeks ago. A foxy little number named Adriana. That's you, darlin'. Don't deny it."

"I'd only met Raptor *that* day and it wasn't all about protecting me. We didn't even know each other."

Mud stared at me, now looking a little uncertain.

An idea began to take shape in my head. "The truth is, he pretty much forced himself into the situation. I was telling Breaker that I wasn't interested in going for a ride with him, when Raptor thought he needed to step in, like some kind of macho idiot. For some dumbass reason, he didn't think that I could handle saying 'no' to Breaker all on my own. The truth is I didn't need his help. I didn't even welcome it."

He leaned forward on the bar, his eyes red and dilated. "Is that right?"

I nodded. "Yes it fucking is. And now, my best friend is dead and I'm being held prisoner. I'm caught in the middle of this so called shit-storm between you and them and I sure as hell shouldn't be. I am *not* Raptor's Old Lady. I'm not even his girlfriend. I couldn't give a shit about him or his gang, the Vipers."

"The Gold Vipers," he corrected.

"Whatever they are," I snapped angrily. "Like I said, I don't give a fuck about them, or you, for that matter. You want to kill each other? Fine. But, don't you dare label me as Raptor's Old Lady."

I wasn't lying either. I didn't give a crap about him anymore, or the Gold Vipers. My friend was dead and my heart was broken.

149

They'd given me nothing but sorrow and pain.

He smiled at my words. "You know, I kind of like you." Mud walked around the bar and strolled over to where I was standing, his eyes boring into mine. "I'm a pretty good judge of character and I can honestly say that I believe every word you just said. You do hate them. Especially, Raptor."

I had to force myself not to look away from his penetrating gaze. "You better believe it. They can fall off the face of the earth, for all I care."

"That's how I feel," he said, his eyes glazed as he watched me. "Now you can understand my frustration, can't you?"

"Totally. They're nothing but a bunch of assholes. Someone needs to take them out," I said, holding my breath after I said it. I wasn't sure if he'd believe I felt that heavily, but I put my best game-face on. "Someone who has the brains and muscle do it. Like you guys."

He moved closer to me and it was a struggle not to back away. Not only was he bigger and much more frightening up close, but Mud smelled like he hadn't showered in days. The whiskey on his breath added to the repulsive stench and I had to breathe through my mouth to keep from gagging.

"You know, when I first saw you tonight, I said to myself – 'How the fuck did a loser like Raptor get lucky with this classy chick?'"

"He never even came close," I said, forcing a smile. "I'm sure he wanted to, but I'd die before letting him touch me."

His eyes searched mine. "I know you're upset about your friend. That shit is all on them, though. You know that? If they wouldn't have hired that fuck, The Judge, to kill Breaker, she'd still be alive. It's their fault that Krystal is dead. Not mine."

I couldn't believe he was insane enough to think that I'd believe the shit coming out of his mouth. "That makes sense," I said.

Before I could protest, he grabbed me by the back of the head and smashed his lips against mine. My first impulse was to push him away as hard as I could, but then I remembered the gun. Using every ounce of willpower I had, I let him shove his tongue into my mouth, and somehow managed not to puke.

Then, I placed my hand on his chest and slid my fingers into the small curls that ran along his upper chest, and tugged on them playfully.

Mud groaned and pulled my hips against his. I could feel his erection pressed against my stomach. He grabbed my hand and placed it over his cock. "Fuck, you turn me on. I need to be inside of you," he said, biting my lip.

Trying not to cry, I closed my eyes. He was such a disgusting human being and I couldn't believe I was allowing him to touch me. I just kept reminding myself that if I could get the gun, everything would be okay.

Mud, who had no idea of the inner turmoil raging inside of me, grabbed my crotch. "I bet you're wet for me, aren't you? You want me as much as I want you?"

"Yes," I whispered, trembling. I slid my other hand over his skin and was about to reach around his back for the gun, when he released me.

"Fuck," he said, moving away from me. He ran a hand along his face and began to pace. "What the fuck am I doing?"

"You were about to get lucky," I lied. "What's stopping you?"

He continued to pace. "I'm fucking higher than a kite. I shouldn't have done all that blow. Makes me think with my dick when I should be thinking with my noggin." He stopped walking and looked at me. "Fuck it. I'm going to take a shower and then I'm going to go balls deep into your sweet little honey-hole. You down with that?"

I gave him a seductive smile. "Very."

"Let's go," he said, grabbing me by the elbow.

"Where are we going?"

"You'll see."

Mud guided me over to a doorway and then opened it. When he turned on the light, I groaned inwardly. It was some kind of a bedroom. There was an unmade queen-sized bed, a television, a DVD player, and a stack of pornos. I could only imagine what kind of things a black light would pick up.

"So, the question is – do you want to wait here or join me when I clean up?"

"I took one earlier" I said quickly, not knowing what else to say. There was no way I was going to let him rape me in the shower. At least if he left me alone in the bedroom, I could try and find another means of escape.

"Okay," he said, as if my excuse made all the sense in the world. "I won't be long." He nodded toward the movies and laughed wickedly. "Help yourself to those if you'd like to start without me."

I laughed. "Maybe I will."

He reached around and grabbed my ass hard.

I gasped.

"Sorry, I just can't wait to take a bite out of this later. After I'm done licking you from head-to-toe. I've been told that I eat pussy better than anyone. You a screamer?"

"I guess you'll just have to find out," I replied, playing along.

He stuck his tongue out and wiggled it. "That get your juices flowing?"

I couldn't believe he was that much of an idiot. "Oh yeah. I'm ready to go 'Muddin'," I joked.

His eyes widened and he laughed. "You're a funny girl. You know why they call me Mud?"

"No. Why?"

His eyes hardened and a coldness spread across his face. "Because it's usually where I bury my enemies."

"Oh," I replied, worried that he'd seen through my ruse. I touched him tentatively on his arm. "I thought it was because you like playing in the mud. I've always enjoyed it myself."

His face changed again. The horny idiot returned and I relaxed. He reached over and cupped my left breast. "You haven't seen anything yet," he said, squeezing it.

I swallowed. "I can't wait. Go take that shower so we can get started."

He rubbed my nipple through the fabric and then let go. "I'll be back soon. I do need to lock the door, darlin'."

Damn. I forced a smile. "Sure. Of course."

His eyes bore into mine. "I'm telling you right now that I don't trust you. Just because you're not a fan of the Gold Vipers," he said, backing away from me, a funny smile on his face. "But, after our little fuck session, I might go easy on you. Hell, I might even let you go. If you want to go, that is. You might enjoy my company more than you think."

"Oh, I'm sure I will," I replied. "There's nothing at home for me anyway."

His smiled widened. "I'll be back in a few minutes and then we'll

153

get started."

"Can't wait," I said, faking a smile so wide that my cheeks began to ache.

He shut the door and locked it from the outside.

Sighing in relief, I turned my attention toward the bedroom. I wasn't sure exactly what I was going to do, but I needed to find a way to escape before that disgusting pig put his hands on me again.

TWENTY FOUR

FOUR

RAPTOR

MY GPS TOLD me that Jensen was just over three hours away. On the way out of town, Tank and I stopped at a gas station, filled our tanks, and grabbed several cans of energy drinks.

"Stay strong, brother," said Tank, holding out his fist.

I tapped it with mine. "Thanks, man. Knowing that you've got my back makes it easier."

He nodded. "I'll always have your back. Just like I know you'll always have mine."

"Damn straight."

We parted and started driving, with me in front and him following in his truck. After thirty minutes of being on the road, my phone rang, jerking me to attention. It was a private number.

"Yeah," I answered.

"Let me guess, you're headed out here to try and save your bitches." It was Mud.

"Let them go," I said, not answering the question. "Those girls have nothing to do with the shit between our clubs. Nothing."

He laughed. "I already know that. Do I care? No."

"You just keep your end of the bargain and we'll keep ours," I lied, glancing at Tank's headlights behind me. Behind him was some kind of sports car and I began to get paranoid. What if we were being followed?

"I get my money and the piece of shit who you douchebags hired to kill Breaker, you'll get your girls back."

"In one piece," I stated flatly.

"Speaking about pieces, that redhead is a hot number. What's it like, tapping that pussy? I might have to find out."

I gripped my hands on the steering wheel. "You fucking touch her and I'll kill you."

He laughed. "Oh, I've already touched her."

"Repeat that?" I growled, wanting to beat the fuck out of him.

"Don't worry, I haven't shown her what a real man is like. Not yet, anyway. But, I have to tell you. She doesn't seem like she's missing you too much. Now, why is that?"

It was obvious. She was still pissed off at me for earlier. But, I also knew that out of the two evils, she'd much rather be in my company than be kidnapped by Mud.

"Raptor? You still there?"

"Yeah," I mumbled, my head racing with images of Mud forcing himself on her. I pressed harder on the gas.

"I think you've really got it for Adriana, don't you?"

"Leave her alone," I threatened. "Or you won't get your money."

His voice hardened. "Listen, I'm the one making up the rules here, not you. Don't forget it, brother."

"I'm not your fucking brother," I growled.

"That's right. The Judge is. Isn't he?"

"What the fuck you talking about?" I said, wondering how he'd come across that news.

"Don't play me for a fool. I've heard all about it. Guess your mother can't keep her legs or her mouth closed."

"Fuck you."

He laughed and hung up.

TWENTY FIVE

ADRIANA

I LOOKED AROUND THE bedroom for a weapon and even checked under the bed, which ended up being a mistake. I found a couple of used condoms and a monstrous dildo that almost caused me to puke. Shuddering, I got back up and walked over to the bedroom door to listen for sounds. Surprisingly, I heard a woman mumbling to herself.

"Brandy?" I said loudly, hoping it was her and she'd gotten loose.

The person went quiet.

"Hello?" I called.

"Hello, who are you?" asked the woman, just outside the door. It was definitely not Brandy.

"Um, my name is Adriana." I twisted the door handle. "I think I've been locked in here by accident."

"Hold on," she replied, unlocking it from the outside.

"Thanks," I replied, glancing at her quickly. She was a tall woman with platinum blonde hair which was pulled into a ponytail, and dark brown eyes.

"I'm April, by the way. Mud lock you in there?" she asked in a low voice.

"Something like that," I replied quickly, walking around her and over to the bar. Knowing that Mud could pop back in at any moment, I began searching for something I could use as a weapon, like an icepick or a knife. What I found was even better – a Remington single-barrel shotgun.

"Where is he?" asked April, looking a little nervous.

"Taking a shower. Why? You his Old Lady?"

Her shoulders relaxed. "Hell no. He's a shithead. I'm here to get some things and leave."

"I like you already," I said, my heart pounding as I checked to see if the gun was loaded, thanking my mother for keeping a similar one in the back of the jewelry shop. I couldn't remember exactly when she'd purchased it, but Vanda had been insistent on having one. She'd even taken gun classes and then taught me the basics, although we'd never fired it ourselves. I'd always thought that the rifle had been a little overkill, but my father's death had scared the hell out of her. Personally, I didn't think she could ever use it, but if it eased some of her fears, that was good enough for me.

April's eyes widened when she noticed the gun. "Whoa, what are you doing with that?" she asked, putting her hands in the air.

Satisfied that the gun was loaded and ready to go, I hurried around the bar. "Relax. I'm trying to save a woman's life," I said, hurrying toward the other hallway where Skull had disappeared with Brandy. When I rounded the corner, I noticed only one doorway. Gripping the gun tightly, I walked toward it and stopped to listen. Inside I could hear music playing.

"That's Skull's bedroom. I wouldn't go in there," whispered April, over my shoulder.

"Oh, I'm going in there. Stand back," I whispered. "So you don't get hurt."

"Sure. Okay," she whispered, backing up. "I hope you know what you're doing."

I didn't but there wasn't any time to work out a better plan. Taking a deep breath, I opened the door as quietly as I could, hoping to surprise them. The first thing I noticed was that Brandy was lying naked and still on the corner of a king-sized bed. Skull appeared to be lying next to her, taking up the better part of it. Curiously, he didn't move a muscle either.

"Oh, my God," I gasped, noticing the blood on the mattress.

"What the hell happened?" asked April, standing behind me again. "Are they on something?"

"I… I don't exactly know," I said, trying to adjust my eyes to the darkness. It was then that I noticed that Skull's eyes were open. He was staring up at the ceiling and not blinking.

"Holy shit, is he dead?" asked April.

"Looks like it," I replied, lowering the gun. I stepped over to Brandy, who I could see was breathing. "Are you okay?" I asked, bending down. There was so much blood on the bed. *Too* much blood. She obviously needed an ambulance.

Instead of answering, Brandy continued to stare blankly at the wall, obviously in shock. Leaning closer, I pushed her hair away from her face to see how bad the bruises were. When I saw the blood on her lips and chin, I felt the hair stand up on the back of my neck.

"Turn on the light," I told April, standing up.

She did and then we both gasped in horror.

Brandy had bitten off part of his testicles and it looked like he'd bled to death. I stumbled to the other side of the bed and threw up.

TWENTY SIX

MUD

S TANDING IN THE shower, Mud's head began to clear. The one above his shoulders. He thought about Adriana, who was definitely one hot piece of ass. But, she was also his prisoner and one whose best friend had been murdered by his orders. It didn't seem logical that she'd be willing to put that aside, much less put out.

Unless… she was a few sandwiches short of a picnic?

Although he would have liked to believe that she was missing some marbles, Mud knew that Adriana wasn't allowing him to jump her bones simply because she wanted him to bang her. She was doing it to save her life and he couldn't blame her. Hell, he even admired such tenacity. This girl was a survivor. One who had enough moxie to do what she had to in order to stay alive. It was just too bad that they'd met in such fucked up circumstances. Not only was she beautiful, but she appeared to have her shit together and there seemed to be a shortage of those types around his neighborhood.

When he finished in the shower, he pulled on a pair of sweats, and walked into his bedroom, which was above the clubhouse. Mud still hadn't purchased a place in Hayward, like most of his brothers had. They seemed to be settling in fine. Then there was his nephew, Skull, who couldn't live by himself, because he was a certified sociopath. The last time he'd rented an apartment by himself, Skull had killed and buried his landlord's body after getting an eviction notice for non-payment of rent. Afterward, Mud let him stay with him, knowing that if he didn't, Skull would end up behind bars and that couldn't happen. He needed his nephew to do the kind of dirty work that most would have trouble doing, like the thing with Krystal. Skull had not only killed her, but had carved a message on her stomach about 'revenge being sweet'. After seeing him do that job, and with such delight, Mud knew that Skull had some issues, but he was not only a Devil's Ranger, he was family. They stuck together, no matter what.

Mud splashed on some aftershave and then headed toward the door. As he gripped the knob, he felt a sudden overwhelming sense of doom and had a suspicion that if he opened up the door, he was as good as dead. It was the kind of feeling that had saved his life a number of times and he knew not to dismiss it. Releasing the handle, he backed up slowly and went for the gun, the one he'd almost stupidly forgotten. As he picked it up, a creak on the other side of the doorway confirmed his suspicion. Someone was standing there. Someone who shouldn't be creeping around. He knew it wasn't one of his boys, they'd have knocked by now. He was pretty sure he'd locked Adriana in the other bedroom, as well. Even if she got out, he doubted she'd run straight into his arms. She'd try to escape. It was someone who wanted to take him by surprise. Probably put a bullet through his head. Mud hadn't heard of any Gold Viper Chapters living in Minnesota, but that didn't always mean shit. They had friends.

With his heart pounding in his chest, he raised the gun, pointed it toward the door, and began firing. On the fourth shot, he heard a loud thud. Grinning triumphantly, Mud waited a few seconds and then moved to the side of the wall next to the door. Cautiously, he reached over and opened it. When no shots were fired back, he jerked around the corner with his gun still drawn, and checked the hallway.

It was empty.

Knowing that it hadn't been his imagination, that he'd actually heard a noise, he kept his gun drawn and crept quietly down the hallway. When Mud reached the exit that led to the stairwell, he took a deep breath and opened it. Not hearing anything, he slipped through the door and began moving down the stairs toward the main part of the clubhouse. When he reached the bottom, he began to have some doubts about the noise he'd heard upstairs.

Maybe the drugs had made him more paranoid than usual?

The shit had been strong and he recalled his supplier, Mad Dog, mentioning that it had been laced with something extra special. He just couldn't recall exactly what the man had said. Knowing that Mad Dog knew what he was doing and always kept his clients coming back for more, he'd accepted it without question. He decided that the next time he bought anything from Mad Dog, it would be straight-up and not mixed with anything.

Relaxing slightly, he opened the door to the clubhouse and stepped inside. Not seeing anything unusual, he made his way over to the room he'd locked Adriana in and opened the door. When he found the room empty, he gritted his teeth angrily.

"Adriana?" he barked out. "Where in the fuck are you?"

There was no answer.

Mud quickly raced down the hallway toward Skull's bedroom. When he opened up the door and saw his nephew's body, he sucked in his breath.

"Crazy fucking bitches," he muttered in disbelief. Skull was naked and lying in a pool of his own blood, which was coming from his mutilated groin. He was obviously dead, which was probably a good thing, considering the cause of death.

Outraged, Mud checked the rest of the clubhouse, and outside, for the girls, but they appeared to be long gone.

Fuck!

They'd not only killed his nephew, his second in command, but they'd escaped. Shaking with anger, he stormed over to the bar and poured himself another whiskey. As he was about to slam it down, the lights flickered off.

"Who's there?" he hollered, crouching behind the bar, his gun raised again.

Someone started whistling a tune and it made the hair stand up on the back of his neck. He raised his head and fired a shot toward the sound. The whistling stopped but Mud wasn't stupid enough to believe that he'd hit a bulls-eye.

"Heard you wanted me," called a deep voice on the other side of the room. "So, here I am."

Mud swore. "That you, *Judge*?" he growled.

"Why don't you stand up and find out? Or, are you missing some of your balls, like that guy in the bedroom?"

He fired the gun toward the voice. "Fuck you, asshole."

"No, you're the one who was fucked the minute you started shooting your mouth off about taking me down," he replied, his voice now in a different location.

"You don't scare me," answered Mud, before racing over to a sofa near the pool table in a crouched position. "Now, why don't you show yourself and we can do this like men."

"Put your gun down and I'd be happy to."

Mud wasn't about to give up his gun, although from his calculations, he was almost out of bullets. He thought about the shotgun, the one he kept under the bar, and swore to himself. He needed to go back there and get it.

"What is it with you, anyway?" said Mud, trying to keep him talking. "You too good for the club life?"

"I don't need it."

"Don't you want to be part of something that means anything? Like the Devil's Rangers?"

"What kind of lies have you been telling yourself? There's nothing special or honorable about your club, Mud."

"Don't talk to me about honor. I live and die for my brothers. They look up to me. They respect me because I steer them right. They fucking chose me as their leader."

"You're nothing."

"Nothing? I'm the fucking president of the Devil's Rangers, Hayward Chapter, motherfucker," he spat. "Me! What are *you*? You're just a pussy gun-for-hire. And what is with that fucking stupid ass road name? The *Judge*."

"I didn't come up with name, but I don't mind it. I guess some think that I bring justice to scumbags like you and Breaker, when the law fails. Getting paid to do it only sweetens the deal."

"Oh, I get it," he laughed. "You see yourself as some kind of crime-fighting vigilante. What a crock of shit. You're no better than any of us. You know it and I know it," he said before creeping back over to the bar.

The Judge didn't respond and Mud smirked. He'd obviously hit a chord. Amused, he reached under the bar, to where he'd kept the shotgun and frowned when he noticed that it was missing.

"The real problem is that you're the one who doesn't know shit," said a voice above him.

Mud jerked his head up and found himself looking into the barrel of the shotgun he'd been searching for. Closing his eyes, he could hear his heart pounding as he waited for a violent end. After a few seconds of nothingness, he opened his eyes, only to find the shotgun sitting on the bar and The Judge gone.

"What the fuck?" he laughed coldly, grabbing the gun. "You could have had me right there."

"Too easy and messy," said his voice, near the exit. "I've had enough of that for one night."

"Too messy?" he hollered and then remembered Skull's body. "You're the one who killed my nephew? Not that little bitch?"

"Negative. I'm the one who killed the both of you," he replied, slipping out of the building.

"What the fuck?" mumbled Mud, standing up. He looked around the room, confused.

SMILING TO HIMSELF, Jordan took the detonator out of his pocket as he headed toward his rental. Without looking back, he pushed the button and the clubhouse exploded.

FIVE MINUTES EARLIER...

TWENTY SEVEN

ADRIANA

I DIDN'T WASTE ANY time getting Brandy out of Skull's bedroom and April was kind enough to help us escape before Mud finished with his shower. Grabbing a blanket from the other bedroom, we wrapped it around her and hurried out of the building. As we reached April's car, I realized that I'd left the shotgun inside.

"Don't you dare go back inside for it," said April. "That's how most people die in movies. Someone going back for something that they think they need but really don't."

"Good point." I turned to look at Brandy, who was staring blankly outside. "We should get her to a hospital. And call the police."

"Are you sure you want to do that? She tore his shit up, you know. Murdered him," said April as she began driving. "Your friend will be the one who gets locked up if they see what she did."

"But they kidnapped us and raped her. She did it out of desperation. They've got to realize that."

"I suppose a lawyer could get her off on some kind of a temporary insanity plea," she replied.

"I didn't do it," whispered Brandy.

I turned back to her. "Brandy. Are you okay?"

Brandy nodded.

"What did you say?" asked April.

She cleared her throat and spoke louder. "I said, I didn't do it. I didn't kill him."

"Girl, I don't know if you realize this, but you bit off part of his nuts and he bled to death. That's what certainly killed him," said April.

She shook her head. "No. A man snuck in when Skull was raping me. The guy put him in some kind of a headlock until he blacked out. Then," she grimaced, "he took the knife and cut him. I can't believe that Skull didn't wake up. It had to have been painful and there was so much blood."

"So that guy who put him in the headlock is the one who cut him in the nuts?" asked April.

"Yes. He also told me not to tell the cops that I'd seen him."

I stared at her in shock. "Are you kidding?"

"No."

"What about your face?" I asked, noticing that we hadn't managed to clean all of the blood off.

Brandy let out a ragged sigh. "I put it there. To make it look like I'd killed him myself."

"Why would you bother with all of that?" asked April, looking horrified.

"I don't know. Maybe because the guy who killed Skull was so nice and I didn't want him to get arrested," she said, staring back outside.

"Nice?" said April, smirking. "I guess he did save her. That was pretty nice."

"Was he a Gold Viper?" I asked Brandy.

"I don't know. I don't think so."

"What did he look like?" I asked, curious.

"The lights were dim, so I didn't see much other than his dark hair. I think he was good looking, too. I'm really not sure about anything else."

"Did he say anything else?" asked April.

"He told me that he was going after Mud, too," she said and then grunted. "Thank God, because Trevor would have never come through for me. Maybe you, but not me."

"Right," I mumbled.

"He hates me," she said miserably.

"Trevor doesn't hate you. It's pretty obvious," I said, frustrated.

"Well he sure doesn't *love* me. Not like you, anyway."

"The man doesn't know what love is." I ran a hand through my hair. "If he did, he wouldn't have had sex with you yesterday," I reminded her.

"We didn't have sex."

It took me a while to respond. "What do you mean?"

"I had sex yesterday, but it was with someone else. A guy that I met at Griffin's. You thought it was me, because I had Trevor's phone."

"What were you doing with his phone?" asked April. She smiled, sheepishly. "Sorry, I don't know who this Trevor is, but I'm already caught up in the drama. I need to know."

I turned back and stared at Brandy in disbelief. "So, it wasn't him?"

She nodded. "I didn't mean to fool you. I swear to God. When I dialed your number, it was completely by accident."

"But, I heard you say his name," I said, confused.

"That's because I wanted it to be him. I *imagined* that it was him." She started to cry. "But it wasn't. I still love him, I can't help it. I'm sorry for being such a bitch. I'm not normally like that."

I couldn't help it; staring at her bruised face and knowing how much she'd been through in the last few hours, my heart went out to her. I reached back and squeezed her shoulder. "It's okay, Brandy."

"No, it's not. It really isn't," she sobbed. "I know how much he loves you and I've been so jealous and pissed off. But, the truth is, I don't deserve him. I cheated on him with so many guys. Not just the ones he knows about either."

"I don't get it, Brandy. Why did you cheat on Trevor like that?" I asked. "If you loved him so much?"

"I don't know. It's like, sometimes I get so turned on by other men that I can't help myself."

"She doesn't love him," said April. "That's why."

"I do," she protested. "But sometimes, I think… I'm actually addicted to sex, especially with strangers."

"So, you're a sex addict?" said April.

She shrugged. "Maybe. I guess it makes sense. I didn't even mind too much about having sex with Skull."

April gasped. "Even when he was raping you?"

"I'm fucked up in the head. What can I say…" she said, looking disgusted with herself.

"You can get help for it," I said. "Treatment."

She smiled grimly. "The truth is, I don't know if I'm ready. I like doing it too much."

"I'm sure many drug addicts feel the same way and that's why they end up with nothing in the end if they don't quit using. Anyway, you need to get help. At least do it for the baby's sake," I said.

"You're pregnant?" asked April, staring back at her through the rearview mirror."

Brandy laughed nervously. "Actually, about that. I'm… I'm not pregnant."

TWENTY EIGHT

RAPTOR

WE WERE JUST entering Minnesota when my phone rang. I recognized the number right away.

"You getting closer to Hayward?" asked Jordan Steele.

"Almost there. Where do you want to meet?"

"About that – it's done. Your women are safe and Mud will never be a problem for you again."

"What do you mean?" I asked, shocked. "I thought we were going to do this together?"

"There wasn't time. The girls were in immediate danger. When I arrived, one was about to be raped by Mud and the other was in the process of it. She'd also been beaten badly. I probably saved her life."

"Which one was of them was being raped and beaten?" I asked, wishing that I'd have had a chance to get my hands on the guy who'd done it.

"The blonde."

"She okay?" I asked, more worried about the baby than of Brandy. I wanted to feel guilty about that knowledge, but I didn't.

"Pretty shaken up. Obviously, she needs to see a doctor."

"Was it Mud?"

"No. It was Skull. They're both taken care of, though."

I sighed. "Well, thank you. We owe you big time."

"No you don't. It had to be done."

"How did you get out there so quickly?"

"Let's just say that I have friends in high places. Including, pilots."

"Lucky you."

"Just so you know, a woman drove the girls away from the building before I blew it up. In case you're wondering where she's at

179

right now."

My eyes widened. "You blew up their clubhouse?"

"Yes. I thought it would clean up any evidence that linked the girls to their deaths. Now you don't have to worry about being implicated either."

"And you know for sure that Mud is dead?"

"If he isn't, then he'll be spending months in a burn ward and the rest of his life recovering. You know, I almost wish he survives. Instant death for a megalomaniac like that is too merciful."

I had to agree. Mud deserved a long, painful death.

"Oh, one more thing before I go, tell Slammer that this one was on me. Just make sure that my name is never linked to Mud's death."

"Did you cover your tracks?"

"What do you think?"

"You obviously know what you're doing."

"Practice makes perfect," he replied, a smile in his voice. "So, little brother, let's get together for the holidays. Get to know each other. Exchange gifts, maybe share a bottle of something smooth."

My eyes widened. "Really?"

"No."

"You don't have many friends, do you?" I asked, smirking.

He chuckled. "Look, it's not that I'm not interested in getting to know you, it's just that it's too dangerous. For both of us."

"I get it."

He was silent for a few seconds and then said, "Keep my number. Use it if you ever run into a situation like this again. I mean it."

"Thanks. No offense, but I'm hoping I never have to use it."

"Me too, kid."

TWENTY NINE

ADRIANA

"WHAT ARE YOU talking about?" I asked, staring at her in shock.

"I'm not pregnant," she said, her voice barely audible. "I never was."

I wanted to reach back there and shake the hell out of Brandy. "What?! How could you lie about something like that?"

"I wanted him back," she said, sadly. "I know it was wrong and everything, but –"

"Didn't you think that he was going to find out?" I snapped. "I mean, what in the fuck were you thinking?"

"I was going to try and get pregnant before he figured it out. But, he kept refusing to sleep with me."

That bit of news made me smile. "He did?"

"I told you, he loves you. Not me."

"I can see why. You're pretty messed up," said April. "No offense."

"I know I am," said Brandy, tears springing to her eyes again. "But, at least I'm trying to come clean."

"About that, why have you had a change of heart? I'd told him to screw off, so it would have just been the both of you. You could have kept this information to yourself and tried to get back with Trevor. If he loved you once, he might fall for you again."

"Maybe it's because I feel guilty now," she replied, wiping her cheeks. "Especially after what you've done for me. You two deserve to be together. He deserves to be with someone like you. Not me."

I sighed.

"Do you still love him?" she asked.

"Yes."

She smiled. "Good. Then telling you the truth was worth it."

"Not to interrupt your conversation," said April. "But, where do you want to go? To the police?"

"No," said Brandy. "We can't. They'll ask us too many questions and I don't want that guy getting arrested."

"What about a hospital?" she asked. "Do either of you need one?"

"No," I replied. "What about you, Brandy? Is anything broken or are you cut, anywhere?"

She touched her nose. "My nose might be broken. It hurts like hell, but I'm afraid to see a doctor in this area. I want to wait until I get home."

"Where exactly are we?" I asked April.

"Hayward, Minnesota."

"Crap. How far from home is that?" asked Brandy.

"Where do you two live?"

"We live in Jensen, Iowa," I replied.

"I don't know how far away that is, to be honest. I suppose I can look it up on my phone. Do you two have any money to get back?"

"No," I replied. "I don't have my ID, either, so I can't have my mother send me cash. Look, if you can loan us some money, I'll pay you back and then some. I swear."

"I don't have much money myself" she said. "But, I can probably drive you home. Hell, I was on my way out of town anyway."

"What were you doing at their clubhouse?" I asked.

"To be honest, I was going to try and steal some money from Mud or Skull before leaving town."

"Why were you leaving?" asked Brandy.

"Do you really have to ask?" she said dryly.

"I think the better question is, why were you friends with him in the first place?" I asked.

"We were never friends. I mean, there was a time when I'd first met him that he actually swept me off my feet, believe it or not. He was fun and playful," her face darkened. "But then I found out what a true asshole he really was."

"How did you meet him?" I asked.

"I met him at a party, a while ago. Then, when his club moved out here to Hayward, we hooked up again." She frowned. "I thought it would be great, hanging out with Mud. But, I was wrong. He hates women. All of them."

"Hopefully Mud doesn't have to worry about them anymore," said Brandy. "I hope he's dead."

"I hope so," said April. "I really do."

I couldn't believe how nonchalant they sounded, talking about a man dying. But, if anyone deserved to be six feet underground, it was Mud.

THIRTY

RAPTOR

FTER HANGING UP with The Judge, I called Tank and told him what had happened.

"So, Mud's dead. What about the girls? Where are they?"

"I don't exactly know."

"Don't you think that Adriana would call her mother, and let her know where she is?"

"Yeah. Good point. I'll call Vanda and see if she's heard from her."

"Why don't we stop somewhere and grab a bite to eat while we figure out what to do next?" said Tank. "I'm tired and need food before I pass out."

"Okay. Next diner or drive-thru we see, we'll stop and grab something."

"Sounds like a plan."

We hung up and I called Vanda. Unfortunately, she hadn't heard from Adriana yet.

"What? She's okay? How do you know?" asked Vanda.

"I just know," I answered.

"You just know," she repeated dryly. "Trevor, that answer isn't good enough for me. If you don't give me proof that my daughter is alive and well, I'm sending the police your way, since you *know* what's going on."

"Don't come down on me, Vanda. I wasn't involved in kidnapping her and I wasn't the one who helped her escape," I said, frustrated. "All I know is that someone called to let me know she was fine. You want more information than that, you'll need to talk to her when she comes home."

"And you trust this individual?"

"Very much," I replied. "Believe me, if he said she's safe, then she is. I just don't know exactly where she is at the moment."

"Wait a second, I have a call coming in," said Vanda, excitedly. "I have to go."

"If it's her, have her call me," I said.

"Okay," she said and then hung up.

I put my phone down and kept driving north. Less than three miles later, we pulled into a truck-stop diner and went inside. As the waitress was pouring me a cup of coffee, my cell phone began to ring. It wasn't a number I recognized, but the voice on the other end choked me up inside.

"Hello, Trevor," said Adriana softly.

I closed my eyes and let out a ragged sigh. "Hello, Kitten."

THREE WEEKS LATER, MAUI

THIRTY ONE

ADRIANA

"**I**S THAT JESSICA?" I asked Trevor, as we stood in line at the Luau. We were in Maui, at Slammer and Frannie's wedding reception. It was shortly after seven o'clock and from where we were standing, you could hear the sound of the ocean waves over the tropical music. Talk about paradise.

Trevor, who I'd actually gotten to wear a black Tommy Bahama camp shirt under his cut, with a pair of white shorts and flip-flops, turned around and looked at the girl I was referring to. "Yeah. That's her."

Jessica, who was sitting next to her mother, the bride, at the main table, looked up and our eyes met. She smiled warmly and I smiled back. I'd seen her at the wedding but hadn't been sure.

"She seems nice," I said, looking back at Trevor. "How is she doing?"

"Okay, I guess," he replied, filling his plate with Kalua Pua'a, which was roasted pork. He handed me the tongs. "Tank's been her shadow for the past couple of days. He's really taken it upon himself to be her new overprotective brother."

"That's sweet of him," I said, grabbing some pork for my own plate. "I know I'd feel protected, having a brute like Tank following me around."

"You don't feel protected with me?" he asked, raising his eyebrows.

"Oh, you know what I mean. I'm just saying that she's in good hands."

"So will you be, later tonight," he replied, smiling wickedly.

A teenaged girl who was standing on the other side of him looked over her shoulder and giggled at us.

"Good going," I whispered, smiling sheepishly at the pink cheeked girl, who quickly looked away. "Now everyone knows what's happening in our hut."

Trevor leaned in to me. "I think they already know, especially after the way I had you screaming last night," he whispered near my ear.

I couldn't help but smile at that memory. If there was one thing he was good at, it was making me scream. Thankfully, it was only in good ways lately.

"Let's go sit over there," he said, pointing to a table away from everyone.

"Don't you want to visit with some of your buddies?" I asked, a little surprised. Most of the Gold Vipers had made the trip with their Old Ladies and were sitting together.

"We have all week to talk. I just want to relax and enjoy your company for a while," he said, grabbing a beer from a bucket of ice.

"Aww..." I replied, staring up at him lovingly. "You must be looking to get lucky again tonight."

"I have to admit, that was in the back of my head, too," he teased as I grabbed a bottle of water.

"Really? Well, don't count your chickens before they're hatched."

"I don't need to. I've got the cock," he whispered. "To get things moving."

I laughed. "You're so full of it."

"I'm surprised it took you so long to figure that out."

"Believe me, I knew it the first time you opened your mouth."

Chuckling, he grabbed my hand and led me over to a picnic table. Putting our plates down, we sat next to each other.

"Talk about paradise," he said, looking toward the ocean. "This is pretty amazing, isn't it?"

"It certainly is," I replied, pushing my hair behind my ears. "I keep wanting to pinch myself, to make sure it's not some kind of a dream."

"You and me both. Especially, after everything that's happened. And now we're here together. In tropical paradise." He smiled. "Damn, if I had the money, I'd never go back to Iowa. Hell, I wish we could stay here forever."

I nodded, still so grateful that we'd been able to pull through all of the obstacles that had tried to separate us, including Brandy. When Trevor had found out that she wasn't pregnant, he'd been so furious that I thought he was going to add to the bruises on her face. But once he'd calmed down and realized that Brandy's lies were just a symptom of a more deeply-rooted problem, one that needed professional counseling, he cut her some slack and even helped pay for the surgery that was needed to fix her broken nose.

"How are you feeling?" he asked as I stared down at my food.

"Fine," I replied. "Very hungry and this pork smells amazing."

"All of the food here has been pretty good," he said. "That mahi-mahi we had last night was out of this world. Never thought I'd like fish until this trip."

I had to agree, the meal had been outstanding. "If we keep eating like this, though, I'm going to have to buy some new clothes before we get back to Iowa. Things are already getting snug."

"That's okay. Vacations are meant for eating and shopping. In fact, let's do some tomorrow. I'll even chip in to buy you some of those colorful muumuu dresses," he teased.

I groaned. "Those shapeless things that the old ladies were wearing on the bus yesterday?"

"Exactly. Every woman needs a muumuu," said Trevor, taking a swig of beer.

I raised my fork in the air. "Fine. I'll just keep eating and not worry about my figure for the rest of the trip."

"You do have an impressive appetite," he replied. "Which is good, because now you look healthy again."

"Healthy? I feel bloated."

Now that we were on vacation, my appetite had returned and neither of us had stopped eating since we'd arrived in Maui. I'd lost some weight during the time Brandy had been living with him, which I'd chalked up to stress, but now, I was finding it harder and harder to button the top of my shorts.

"You probably just have gas. If you want to feel better, just go ahead and let one rip." He gave me a goofy smile. "There's a good tropical breeze blowing away from us. Nobody will know."

I smirked. "Believe me, I've already tried it."

"I thought that was you earlier," he joked. "Good push, by the way."

Laughing, I elbowed him in the ribs. "I didn't fart around you. That was manure from that horse pulling the couple in the carriage. I even pointed it out to you."

"Now who is full of it? Even a horse couldn't have made that smell. Nice try, blaming it on some poor nag."

"Oh, my God… It wasn't me! I swear."

Trevor roared with laughter. "I'm just teasing you, Kitten. I love watching you get all flustered."

I groaned. "Your sense of humor… I don't know."

"You still love me and you know it."

I leaned over and kissed him. "Of course I do."

"Speaking of 'I do', aren't you glad that I talked you into flying out here to see Slammer get married?"

I nodded. "Yes. I almost didn't make it. My mother was set against me flying out here."

"I know she was."

After we'd returned to Iowa and Trevor had driven me home, my mother had cried for hours, all the while trying to convince me to never see him again.

"He saved my life," I reminded her.

"He's the one who endangered your life in the first place," she countered, frustrated that I still wanted to see him.

"It really wasn't that bad," I replied, the lie sounding pathetic even to me.

"Not bad?! You were kidnapped. The neighbors saw it all! For God's sake, Adriana, nobody thought they'd see you alive again, including me. It was one of the worst nights of my life."

Mine too.

Fortunately, there was one upside to the entire ordeal – it had brought Trevor and I back together. I could still remember that morning, when we'd reunited somewhere between Iowa and Minnesota. We'd met up with them at a diner, and he'd swept me off of my feet. Literally.

"I'm so sorry, Kitten," he said, his voice full of emotion. "This should have never happened to you."

"It's okay," I whispered, feeling such relief in his arms

"Mud will never bother you again. I promise you that."

"I sure the hell hope not."

"He can't. He pissed off the wrong people. He's already been dealt with."

"I believe it," I said before telling him about what had happened to Skull. *"The man who did it obviously got to Mud as well."*

Trevor had confirmed to me that they'd sent the stranger to help rescue us and how important it was to keep him a secret. I promised not to say anything and in the end, after giving the police a vague description of the men that had taken me and leaving out both Brandy and April's names, the cops weren't able to do much more than fill out a police report. All they really knew was that I'd been kidnapped and dropped off on HWY 35, just north of the Minnesota state line.

"Why did they let you go?" asked one of the cops.

"I have no idea. Maybe they had a change of heart or just realized that they'd eventually get caught?"

I could tell that they didn't believe either of my theories, but since I was home and unscathed, they decided to let it go.

"I know," said Trevor, after plopping a piece of pineapple into his mouth. "Who can blame her, though? Three weeks ago you were kidnapped by a group of bikers. Now, you're stuck on an island, far away from her reach, with more of them. She must be going nuts right now."

I laughed. "This is quite different."

"Oh, I don't know. I might kidnap you myself. Lock you in our hut and have my way with you the entire rest of the trip."

I raised my eyebrow. "And skip that snorkeling excursion you've been obsessing about? The one we're supposed to go on tomorrow?"

"Okay, maybe we can take a small break for that," he replied, his eyes sparkling in the moonlight. "Since you're so bent on snorkeling."

I laughed. "Right."

Trevor had been talking about it for days, so excited to try it. Neither of us had ever snorkeled and now I was even looking forward to getting my feet wet.

We spent the rest of the night enjoying the ambience of the luau and talking about what I wanted to do after I finished college.

"What I'd really like to do is find a job and hopefully move out of my mother's place," I told him.

"I think you should move in with me," Trevor said. He had been asking me to for the last week, and now that Brandy had moved out, it seemed like an interesting idea. But, I also knew that it was a little too soon, at least in regards to my mother. With the difficult time she was having with us dating, especially after the kidnapping, I could only imagine her reaction of me moving in with him.

"I can't. At least not now. It's just too soon after everything that's happened. I don't want to rush into it, you know?"

As usual, he just nodded and told me that he understood, which made me love him even more. I could tell that he was used to getting his way, especially with women, but he was being very patient with me.

"Thanks," I said, staring at him. A tropical breeze blew his hair back and away from his face. With his blonde hair, golden tan, and clear blue eyes, I couldn't remember him looking any more handsome.

"For what?"

"For not being pushy."

He grabbed my hand and rubbed my knuckles with his thumb.

"I'm willing to do whatever it takes to keep you in my life for the long haul, Kitten. If giving you space is what you need right now, it's all yours. I'm just happy that you agreed to be my woman and wear my cut. You know how much that means to me."

"I know," I replied.

He'd presented me with it the week before, asking if I'd take on the title of being his Old Lady. His one and only. But, I had made a couple of things clear. I'd be his Old Lady, but I had demands of my own – no other girlfriends or club whores on the side. He agreed and promised to never cheat on me, expecting the same on my end as well. It was an easy promise for me since I couldn't imagine being with anyone else.

We finished eating and then went for a stroll along the beach. It was a beautiful night, with the waves rolling in and the stars twinkling above.

"Question – have you ever been skinny dipping?" he asked when we reached a part of the beach that was private.

"No," I replied.

He grinned wickedly. "Then we'd better pop your cherry."

"What if we get caught?" I replied, intrigued with the idea.

"Have you not noticed how far we've walked?" he said. "Nobody is going to catch us, unless we've been followed, which we haven't."

I looked backward and found that he was right. Not only had we moved far from the luau, but we were also well past the strip of hotels along the beach. I figured that were now on private property because of the houses nearby, but it didn't look like anyone was home.

"Come on, let's do it," he said, removing his cut.

"What about sharks?" I said, staring toward the water.

"Relax. We're not going to see any sharks."

"Famous last words," I mumbled.

"If you're that nervous, we don't have to go very deep."

As usual, I relented for Trevor. "I can't believe you're making me do this."

"You say that a lot."

I smirked. "Yeah, I've noticed. You're a bad influence."

"But a *good* bad."

I chuckled. "A very *good* bad, if there is such a thing." With my back to him, I began to remove my blue and white sundress, when I felt his hands slide around my waist.

"Let me help you," he murmured, his warm lips on my neck. He raised the dress over my head and dropped it into the sand, leaving me standing in only my panties and white strapless bra. His hands cupped my breasts and he pulled me against his chest, which was now also naked. Feeling his hardness pressed against my butt, I closed my eyes and moaned as one of his hands slid down to my panties and began rubbing my clit through the fabric.

"That's it, Kitten. Purr for me," he whispered, pushing my bra up. Nibbling on my neck, Trevor took my nipple between his two fingers and pulled on it playfully. The mixture of pleasure and pain made me even wetter. I threw my head back, thrusting my breasts out so he'd pull on the other one, too. He went for it, pulling and squeezing the nub, sending delicious tingles all the way to my crotch.

"Fuck, you're so sexy," he growled, sliding his hand under my panties. He slipped a finger inside of me and began strumming my clit again.

"Make love to me," I moaned, as he slid another finger inside.

"Patience," he murmured, teasing me by rubbing his cock against my ass. It felt so hard and I imagined it inside of me, thrusting in and out while I met his rhythm with my own.

"You make it hard to have patience," I said, turning around.

Trevor pulled me against him and kissed my lips hungrily then he moved to my breasts, his tongue and mouth warm and wet. Closing my eyes, I slid my fingers into his long, blonde hair, enjoying the softness as he rolled my nipple between his teeth. As he moved to the other one, he dropped his hand to my mound again.

"You going to come for me on the beach, tonight, Kitten?"

"Fuck me and I will," I whispered, touching the hard outline of his cock through his shorts.

Releasing my breasts, Trevor got down to his knees and pulled my panties to the side, exposing my slit. Then, he grabbed me by the hips and pulled me down until I was sitting on his face. Staring up at me, he began stroking my clit with his tongue.

"Oh, my God," I gasped.

"Pinch your nipples," he ordered, pushing my hand up to my breast. "I want to see it."

Trevor loved it when I touched myself, no matter if it was my breasts or other parts of my body. Sometimes he made me masturbate in front of him, which had been intimidating at first. I'd never admitted to doing it, let alone having a man watch me. But, in the end, I found it a real turn-on myself, knowing that he was excited by watching me do it.

I began pulling at my nipples, the way he had while he continued to suck and lick me down below. Every part of me was aching for release as well as his hard cock. Needing to feel it, I reached behind me and unbuttoned his shorts. When I finally had it in my hand, he gasped in pleasure and shoved his tongue deep inside of my hole.

"Yes," I moaned as he did it again, his nose brushing against my swollen clit. "That… feels so good."

He wiggled his nose between my slit with more intensity, and then thrust his tongue back in, noticing what it was doing to me. He repeated the process over and over, until I was screaming out an orgasm and nearly smothering him in the process. When I finally became still, he chuckled and flipped me over. "My turn," he said, pushing his shorts down.

Lying on my back, I stared up at him as he plunged into me, both of our eyes locked together.

"I love you so much, Adriana," he said, pulling out and then moving back in slowly. "I hope you know that."

"Yes and… I love you, too," I replied, wrapping my legs around his waist.

"The sand is a little hard on the knees," he said after a few more thrusts. "Hold on to me tightly."

Not sure what he was planning on, I did what he asked.

Trevor stood up and began carrying me toward the ocean.

"What are you doing?" I asked, as he stepped into the water.

"Taking you skinny-dipping," he said, moving deeper. "Just like we planned."

The water was cool, but pleasant, and the moment we were

waist-deep, he pulled his hips back and began fucking me again. It was a little awkward at first, but after a while, we figured out a rhythm, and as our bodies splashed against each other, I realized how much I enjoyed skinny-dipping.

"Is it safe to come inside of you?" he breathed into my ear.

"Yes," I replied.

Ever since he'd had the scare with Brandy, staying childless seemed to be in the back of his head. He knew that I was on the pill, but it still didn't make him any less cautious. Normally, he even wore a condom.

Trevor stiffened up and held me tightly as he came, one hand buried in my hair, the other holding me against his chest. When he was finished, he kissed me again and then released me.

"This isn't so bad now, is it?" he asked, after we swam out a little further.

"Not bad at all. Glad you talked me into it," I replied, looking back toward the beach. My smile fell. "Hey, who is that by our clothes?"

He turned and scowled. "It's Tank. What in the hell is he doing?"

"It looks like he's leaving with our clothes," I said, staring at him in horror as he began walking back toward the luau with them.

"Hey!" hollered Trevor, swimming quickly toward the shore. "Brother, what the fuck you doing?!"

Tank turned around and waved the clothing in the air, a shit-eating grin on his face. "What? You need these?"

I watched Trevor walk out of the ocean, buck-naked and he reminded me of some kind of sea god, with his long blonde hair and muscular physique, shimmering under the moonlight. He looked so incredible that even his perfectly sculpted ass looked like it was carved out of stone. I smiled as I pictured him cracking walnuts with his hard cheeks.

"Enough of the shit!" hollered Trevor, now chasing Tank around in the sand, who was laughing his ass off. He said something to Trevor and soon both of them were giggling like a couple of kids. Eventually, Tank gave up the game and handed him back our clothing. Then he waved at me, and I waved back.

"Come on out!" hollered Tank. "We won't bite!"

"I think I'm safer out here, with the sharks," I hollered back, laughing.

"Speaking of, isn't that a fin?" called Trevor.

I jerked my head around to look. "Where?!"

They both started laughing again.

"That's not funny!" I hollered, flipping them off.

"Oh, shit! Not the finger!" yelled Tank.

"Trevor is getting more than that when I get out of here!"

"Lucky man! I'll take off so you can beat his ass. Have a good night!" he yelled and then shook hands with Trevor, who was getting dressed. After exchanging a few more words, Tank took off and I eventually got out of the water.

"So, what was that all about?" I asked, pulling my panties on.

"Oh, Tank's three-sheets to the wind," said Trevor, handing me my dress. "He was just having fun."

"How in the heck did he find us all the way over here?"

"Who do you think told me about this spot?" he replied, smiling wickedly.

"Tank's already been here?" I asked, surprised. "With who?"

"Last night he met up with one of the islanders and she showed him this area. I guess those houses on the beach are rental properties," he said, pointing toward the nearest ones. "I guess, right now, nobody is using them."

"No wonder the cops haven't arrested us yet," I said dryly.

He smiled. "I wish I'd have known about them, we could have rented a private house on the beach instead of staying at the resort. Skinny-dip every night before bedtime. Run around naked for the next six days."

"Wait a second, this was all planned?" I said, raising my eyebrows. "Our little rendezvous?"

"The swimming was. Not the sex part. That was a great bonus. I was hoping it would turn into something like that, though. I'm not going to lie."

I grunted.

He stared at me. "Are you angry?"

"No. Why would I be angry?"

"I don't know. I just want to make sure you're cool with what just happened on the beach. I know you're a little modest when it comes to sex."

"Actually, it made it even more enjoyable. I kind of like having sex outdoors," I answered, picking up my flip flops. "It's going to be hard topping a round of sex that exhilarating."

"Sounds like a challenge."

"Does it?"

He grabbed my hand. "Fuck yeah. I can't wait to beat it."

"Think you can?"

He grabbed me and kissed me hard. "Woman, you know I can."

And he did.

Over and over.

For the next six days.

THIRTY TWO

ADRIANA

WE STAYED IN Hawaii for a week, having the time of our lives. Our days were filled with shopping and island excursions, like the snorkeling trip, along with a couple of other activities that Trevor had surprised me with. We even flew over to the Big Island of Hawaii one day, and received a guided helicopter tour of the volcanos. Another time, we went sailing on a yacht with Slammer, Tank, Frannie, and Jessica, who eventually opened up to me. We had a lot in common and I could tell she was relieved to meet someone who shared a lot of similar interests. At the end of the sailing trip, we exchanged phone numbers and promised to get together some evening, when we returned to Iowa.

Evenings on the island were just as wonderful as the days and we usually hooked up with other members of the Gold Vipers for dinner and sometimes dancing. As I got to know each one of them, and the ladies in their lives, I began to understand Trevor's love and commitment toward Slammer, his club brothers, and the kind of lifestyle they'd chosen. Even though I was still pretty shy around them, I began to feel like I was accepted, especially by the other Old Ladies. They even began to call me Kitten, which Trevor said was now my Road Name.

When the trip was over and we returned to Jensen, it was snowing and the roads were bad.

"I'll call you after I get home," said Trevor, as the airport limo service dropped me off at my mother's house. He'd helped me bring my luggage into the foyer and I felt sad, knowing that I wasn't going to be sleeping in his arms that night; I was already missing Trevor and our hut in Maui.

"Okay," I said, not wanting him to leave. My eyes filled with tears and I suddenly felt a little foolish for being such a sap.

He stared into them. "Are you okay?"

I nodded and smiled. "I just had so much fun. It's kind of sad to know that it's over."

"There will be more trips and more excitement," he said, smiling. He leaned over and gave me a kiss. "I promise."

"I know."

He pulled back and stared at me, his eyes a little sad now, too. "Kitten, you look exhausted. You should really get some sleep. I didn't let you do much of it in Hawaii."

I laughed. "I didn't want to. I mean, who wants to sleep when there's so much to do in such a beautiful place? I feel like we could have stayed two more weeks and we'd still miss out on something."

"I know what you mean. We definitely have to go back."

I nodded.

"Who knows, maybe we'll go back there some day and get married," he said, smiling at me.

My heart swelled. "You and I? Married? Out there?"

He laughed at my excitement. "Yeah, or maybe a different island, since I'd feel a little tacky copying Slammer's wedding. Hell, maybe we'll just get married in Jensen and have our honeymoon in Hawaii. It could just be you and me next time. It would probably be much more romantic."

I squealed. "Really?"

"Really."

I threw my arms around Trevor and hugged him close. "I love you so much," I whispered.

"I love you too, Kitten," he whispered back, our foreheads pressed against each other.

We stayed like that for a couple more seconds and then Trevor pulled away. "I have to go before the driver tacks on more charges," he said.

"Okay. Call me."

"Oh, you know I will."

After he left, I called my mother, who was at the shop, to let her know I was back.

"How was it?" she asked.

"Like I told you yesterday, it was amazing," I said, unbuttoning my jacket. "We can't wait to go back."

"So, you're already planning on more trips with him," she said, sounding less than thrilled.

"Yes. Mom, why can't you just lighten up? Trevor is a great guy. He loves me and I love him," I said, wanting her to understand how important he was to me.

"Oh, now it's love?"

I groaned. "Yes, it is. Why can't you just be happy for us?"

"I will once he grows up and gets away from that gang."

"They're nice people and you just don't understand," I said, giving up. "Look, I'm tired from the flight and I don't have the energy to do this right now. What time are you getting home?"

"We're open later, because of Christmas, remember? I should be home after ten. Can you work tomorrow?"

"Yes. Of course."

"Oh good. What about your classes?"

"They don't resume until January," I told her.

"Okay. Do you want me to bring you home something to eat?"

My stomach rumbled at the mention of food. "Sure."

"What would you like? Tacos? Burgers?"

"Both?" I said, chuckling. "There wasn't much to eat on the flight."

"There is some leftover lasagna in the refrigerator," she said. "I had Jim over for dinner, yesterday."

"Oh, great. I'll just eat that," I said, my mouth already watering.

"You sure you don't want me to pick up anything?"

"I'm sure. Don't bother with the fast food. Just get home. The roads are bad, so be careful," I said, looking outside at the snow, which was falling harder than when we'd left the airport. "Our driver had a difficult time keeping it on the road, and it's starting to snow even harder than before."

"I will be careful," she said.

After we hung up, I went into the kitchen and warmed up a large plate of lasagna. When I was finished with that, I heated up a bag of popcorn in the microwave because I was still hungry. As I waited for it to pop, I touched my thickening stomach and sighed. If I kept stuffing my face, I'd have to move up to the next pant size.

It's just your period, I told myself. *You're just getting bloated.*

I hadn't had it yet, but I'd just ended another cycle of birth control pills and knew that it was due any day. I thought about the pregnancy test I'd purchased, when I'd been so sick the month before, and was glad that I hadn't opened it. Whatever had been ailing me seemed to have disappeared around the time of my kidnapping. Now I could return it and get my money back. Twelve bucks was twelve bucks.

I poured the bag of popcorn into a large bowl and grabbed a bottle of water. Taking it up to my bedroom, I set it on the dresser and changed my clothes. When I was comfortable and in my pajamas, I turned on the television and started flipping through the channels. A few minutes later, my cell phone rang.

"Hi, Kitten. Miss me yet?"

"Yes," I told Trevor. "I've been drowning my sorrow in food. I just had a large plate of lasagna and now I'm eating popcorn."

He laughed. "Did I mention that I loved the fact that you have such a hearty appetite?"

"Yes, a few times." I shoved another piece of popcorn into my mouth. "I never used to eat like this, though. It's kind of weird, actually." I sighed dramatically. "It must be that I'm in love. My feelings for you are going to ruin my figure. Thanks a lot."

"I doubt that anything could ruin your figure."

"Have I told *you* lately that I love you?" I replied between bites of popcorn.

He chuckled. "Are you still eating?"

"Yes. I told you. I made some popcorn. I keep getting the munchies."

"Have you been smoking something illegal that you want to tell me about?"

I laughed. "Gosh, no."

He was silent for a few seconds.

"Hello? You still there?"

"Do you think that you could be pregnant?" he asked quietly.

There was no laughter in his voice, this time, and I could almost hear the crickets chirping in the background.

"Don't even go there," I said, feeling suddenly anxious. "Anyway, I'm on the pill. I've told you that."

"It's not one-hundred percent affective, you do realize that."

"Don't worry. I'm *not* pregnant," I repeated, remembering the conversation we'd had on Maui. He'd told me that he wanted to have at least three children, but not until he was in his thirties. "I wouldn't do that to you."

"Kitten, I *want* you to do that to me. Someday, when we're both ready. You know how I feel about kids."

"I know."

"I want a big family and believe it when I say that I want *you* to have my babies. I want to grow old with you and spoil the hell out of our grandchildren. You feel me?"

"Yes."

"But, if you were to get pregnant at any time, I'd man up and take care of you both. I love you, Adriana. More than anything."

Tears sprang to my eyes. "I love you, too," I said, my voice hoarse.

He chuckled. "You crying?"

"No," I replied, reaching over to my nightstand. I grabbed a tissue and wiped my eyes. "Of course not. It's allergies."

"Jesus, yes you are. Do us a favor and buy a pregnancy test," he said. "So I know whether or not I need to start saving for a college fund."

"I'm not pregnant," I reassured him. "Really."

"Glad you're confident about it but you should take one of those tests, though. Just in case."

"As a matter of fact, I have one."

"You do?"

I explained how I'd been throwing up a few weeks ago and had considered the possibility.

"And you never bothered to let me know that you were worried enough that you went to the drugstore and purchased a pregnancy test?"

"There was so much going on at the time. There was that thing with Brandy, and then I was kidnapped and held hostage by the Devil's Rangers," I replied. "It's not like it was on the top of my head at the time."

"Do me a favor and take the test. We'll both feel better."

"I'm not pregnant," I said. "You'll see."

AN HOUR LATER, I stared at the pregnancy stick in horror. There was a blue plus-sign. Per the pamphlet on the box, it was an indication that I was indeed pregnant.

"I am *not* pregnant," I growled, grabbing another test stick to try again. Less than three minutes later, after peeing on the damn thing and almost dropping it into the toilet because my hand was shaking so badly, I tested positive again.

I called Trevor back.

"Well?" he asked.

I started to cry.

"Oh, Kitten."

THIRTY THREE

RAPTOR

"IT'S GOING TO be okay," I told her, feeling a mixture of fear and pride that the woman I loved was carrying my child.

"No," she sobbed. "I'm so sorry. Maybe we should have it terminated."

"What? No. No fucking way," I told her, horrified that she'd even suggested it. "How can you even say that?"

"I didn't mean it," she said, sniffling. "I just wanted to see how you'd respond."

I groaned. Women and their fucking mind games.

"I'm sorry," she repeated again. "I was on the pill. I really was. I mean I tried, you know?"

"It's going to be okay," I said, reassuring both of us. "It's going to work out. We'll get hitched, you can move in with me, and we'll take care of the baby together. You'll quit school and be a fulltime mom."

"Quit school?!" she shrieked. "I can't quit school."

"Okay, that's fine, too. Don't quit school. We'll figure this shit out. Just, calm down."

"I can't believe this," she mumbled, blowing her nose. "I'm too young to have a kid. Twenty-one?"

"Doesn't your friend have one?" I asked, remembering her telling me about it. "She might be able to give you some advice."

"Yeah, Monica." She started crying again. "What are we going to do? We can't afford this right now. You even said –"

"Fuck what I said. Guys always say that because they know how much kids cost and it cuts into their play money. Don't worry, Kitten, we've got this."

"We do?"

"We do," I insisted.

AFTER I HUNG up with Adriana,

I called Tank and told him the news.

"No fucking way. You were just starting to adjust to the fact that you weren't going to be a father. Jesus, you must be pissed."

"I'm not… pissed," I said. "I love Adriana. You know that. So, we're having a baby earlier than we wanted. It is what it is."

"You actually want kids?" asked Tank, surprised.

"Yeah, of course I do. Don't you?"

"Maybe when I'm sixty," he said, laughing. "I'll need to start thinking about who's going to take care of me when I hit those golden years. Until then, I'm wearing a rain suit when I'm in the trenches."

"Rain suits can get holes."

"Then maybe I'll start doubling-up," he said. "Or stay in back, where it's safe."

Laughing, I shook my head.

"I'm just giving you shit," said Tank. "Congratulations, brother. I'm happy for you both."

"Thanks. I appreciate it."

"So, are you going to put a ring on her finger now?"

"Definitely. I want to do this right."

"Make sure you buy it from Vanda, or she's going to be pissed as all hell."

"She's going to be pissed, no matter what," I said, not looking forward to that conversation.

"She'll get over it. By the way, what was that chick's name who helped Adriana and Brandy escape? The one with the big melons?"

"I think her name was April," I said. "Why?"

"I turned on the news, when I got home, and apparently, her brother was found murdered. I recognized a picture of her when they flashed it across the scene. She's wanted for questioning."

"Really?"

"Yeah. April moved away from Hayward, didn't she?"

"She left the night they escaped. From what Adriana says, she'd had enough of Mud and the rest of the Devil's Rangers."

"They must be trying to find her."

"That's what I'm thinking."

"Do you think they blame April for the club being blown up?"

"No, I'm sure they know that we were involved."

"Yeah. You're right. Well, fuck, they'll be retaliating again. Once they pull their shit together. Hell, I'm surprised they haven't done it yet."

"Nobody saw anything out of the ordinary when we were gone?"

"No. We checked in every day. Nothing strange," said Tank.

Not all of our club members had joined us in Maui for Slammer's wedding, including three prospects that were guaranteed membership after volunteering to keep an eye on the clubhouse, as well as Griffin's. They'd also hired extra security for backup, because Slammer knew that the prospects were still wet behind the ears and might underestimate our enemy.

"You'd better keep a close eye on Adriana," said Tank. "Does she own a gun?"

"I don't think so," I replied, remembering the night she'd freaked out on me when I'd pulled a gun on the asshole who'd tried raping her.

"She should. Maybe she'll be open to carrying one around after that business in Hayward."

"I'll talk to her."

"What about Brandy? Where did she disappear to?"

"I think she went to her mother's. I haven't spoken to her since she moved out."

"She might be in trouble, too. All three girls need protection. Anyone know where April went?"

"I don't know. Adriana wasn't even sure. If I remember correctly, though, April mentioned heading south, but I don't think she really knew where she was going."

"Someone will locate her unless she's picked up some new identification. Too bad, she was a beautiful girl." He sighed. "I should have gotten her number. We could have warned her."

"I'm a little surprised that you didn't."

"I was exhausted at the time. Not thinking clearly."

"The one time you should have been thinking with your dick and you weren't."

"I'll try to make sure he thinks harder next time." He laughed at his own pun.

Grunting, I looked at the clock. It was almost eleven and I was still feeling jet lag. "I'm crashing. I'll meet you at the clubhouse tomorrow. Around ten?"

"We have church at three. You knew that, didn't you?"

"Yeah. Slammer already told me."

"You can drop the news to everyone. About the kid."

"Maybe we'll wait until she's farther along. Just in case there's a problem," I said.

"What kind of problem?"

"You know. Like a miscarriage or something."

"She won't miscarriage," said Tank. "Adriana seems like a strong woman. Just watch how hard you fuck her."

My eyes widened. "Is that a danger?"

"I think so. Wait, you're supposed to be gentle in their *last* trimester."

"What's a trimester," I asked.

He explained.

"How in the hell is it that you, of all people, know about this shit?" I asked him.

"They were talking about it on this program called 'The Doctors'."

"Let me guess, daytime television?"

"Yeah."

"Brother, you need to get off of that couch more."

"Believe it or not, I was riding my elliptical when I watched it," he replied, chuckling.

"When did you get an elliptical?"

"A few weeks ago. Hey, someone else is calling me. I'll talk to you tomorrow."

"Sounds good."

After we hung up, I called Slammer, worried about Adriana's safety.

"You heard, huh?"

"Yeah," I said. "Obviously, it's the Devil's Rangers."

"We don't know for sure and I told Tank not to jump to any conclusions, but you know him."

"So, you don't think they're involved?" I said, surprised that he wasn't too worried about it himself. Slammer was the one who usually jumped to conclusions.

"I don't know, but when the remaining members of Mud's Chapter try to avenge Mud's death, they'll be coming after us."

"And our women," I mumbled.

"They're being watched right now. Any of them cross the Iowa border, I'll get a phone call."

"Good."

"Now, stop worrying and get some sleep."

"See you at church tomorrow."

"Don't be late," he said, and then hung up.

THIRTY FOUR

ADRIANA

AFTER I HUNG up with Trevor, I took a shower to try and calm my nerves. I stood under the warm water and closed my eyes, imagining my mother's expression when I informed her that she was going to be a grandmother. I'd always pictured it to be a happy time, but this would not be the case, especially with Trevor being the father. Obviously, she was going to freak out but there really was no way around it. I decided to wait a few days, however, until I got used to the idea myself first.

I slid my hands over my stomach, surprised at my own stupidity. There was definitely a fullness there that wasn't normal. I'd been chalking it off as needing to do more sit-ups and cutting back on late-night snacks, but now that I knew I was pregnant, it all made sense.

I thought about the baby growing inside of me, and wondered if it would be a boy or a girl. I pictured Trevor as a child and couldn't help but smile at the image. Something told me that he was going to be a wonderful father, which made everything a little easier to swallow. As for myself, I've never had much experience around babies. They'd always made me nervous, which was one of the reasons why I never took up babysitting as a teenager. Now I was going to have my own child and I didn't even know how to change a diaper. I was going to be leaning on my mother a lot for support. I only hoped that she'd forgive us by the time the baby was born.

After the shower, I slipped into an over-sized T-shirt and a pair of boxers, then I grabbed my laptop computer and started surfing the web to learn more about being pregnant. As I was reading up on fetus growth, I heard my mother pull into the garage. I quickly shut down my computer and went downstairs to greet her.

"Adriana," she smiled, pulling me into her arms. "I've missed you so much."

"I missed you, too," I said, breathing in her familiar scent of perfume. It was something that she'd worn since I was little and always comforted me.

She pulled away slightly and studied my face. "You certainly look like you've been on vacation, with that tan. Your skin is just glowing."

"I just got out of the shower," I said nervously, remembering that I'd read something about how pregnant women glowed, especially in their second or third trimester. "That's probably why I'm glowing so much."

Her eyes went to my hair. "I know, but your tan is reminding me that I haven't been anywhere tropical in a very long time."

"You're going away with Jim on that trip still, aren't you?"

"It's just a weekend, although, now he's been talking about going on a cruise."

"A cruise? You should, Mom! You deserve a vacation. You work so much and you know that we can handle the store when you're gone."

She smiled. "I know, but it's just a bad time to go."

"A bad time to go? Why?"

She hung her coat up. "After what just happened."

My eyes widened. "You mean with me being kidnapped? That has come and gone. You don't need to worry about me."

"I don't feel comfortable leaving you alone. I mean, what if they come back for you?"

"Mom, nobody is coming back for me, okay? Don't worry about me and think of yourself for a change."

She patted me on the shoulder and walked toward the kitchen. "Easier said than done. Someday, when you have children, you will understand."

Her words gave me goosebumps.

"Are you still hungry?" she called.

"No. I've already eaten some of that lasagna," I replied. "Thanks, by the way. It was delicious."

"You're welcome," she replied, disappearing into the kitchen.

Sighing, I followed her, to let her know that I was going to bed.

"By the way, I've invited Jim over for Christmas Eve," she said.

"Isn't the shop open, that day?"

"Only until four."

"That's earlier than usual," I said, surprised. She usually kept the shop open until eight on Christmas Eve, for shoppers who needed to buy last minute gifts.

"I know, but Jim and I were talking and both of us agreed that there is no reason why we should be at the store, working so late on Christmas Eve. From now on, I'm closing early on that day."

"What about the extra sales from those last minute shoppers?"

"Sometimes it's not about the money, but about family. This year, I want everyone at the shop to spend more time with the people that mean the most to us, because you don't always know how long you'll have with them," she said, looking at me. There was a sadness in her eyes and I had a feeling that she somehow knew that I would be moving out soon.

"Okay," I replied. "You know that I certainly won't complain."

I usually helped her close the store on that day. Now that Trevor was in my life, the last thing I wanted was to be stuck at the shop any later than I had to.

"If you want to invite Trevor over for dinner that night, you can certainly do so," she said, forcing a smile.

"I'll have to see what he has planned," I replied, happy that she was trying, at least.

"You don't know yet?"

"No."

We hadn't even talked about it. On Thanksgiving, he'd spent most of the day at Slammer's and I'd stayed home with my mother, who'd made a giant turkey. It had just been the three of us – Jim, Mom, and me. Afterward, we'd met back at Trevor's and spent the rest of the night, burning off the calories by having wild, passionate sex. It was one of the best Thanksgivings I'd ever had.

"I'm making prime rib with all of the fixings that you love," she said. "You *are* planning on having dinner here, aren't you?"

"Of course," I replied, knowing that if I made other plans, she'd be heartbroken. We always spent it together, usually alone. This year, both of us had new men in our lives and next year, things would change yet again. The thought of buying Christmas presents for my son or daughter, brought a smile to my face.

"What is it?" she asked, noticing my grin.

I looked at her. "I'm just looking forward to the holidays."

"Does Trevor spend much time with his family during Christmas?"

"No," I replied. I filled her in on the kind of parents that Trevor grew up with and I could tell from her expression, she felt bad for him.

"I guess that might explain a little more about why he joined a motorcycle club."

"They really *are* like one big family," I said. "I really got to know a lot of them in Maui and they are nice people. You should really give them a chance."

She nodded but didn't say anything.

I yawned. "Well, I'm going to bed."

"Goodnight," she said, grabbing a bottle of wine out of the refrigerator.

"Since when have you started drinking wine?" I asked, surprised.

Vanda grabbed a glass from the cupboard. "This is just to help me sleep. I need something to unwind. Would you like some?"

It actually sounded good, but I had to watch myself, now that I was pregnant. "No, thanks."

She began opening the bottle. "Okay. If you change your mind, help yourself."

"Okay, thanks Mom," I said, leaving kitchen.

"Goodnight," she called out again.

I went upstairs and slid into bed. As I drifted off to sleep, I imagined Trevor dressed in a Santa-suit, with our son sitting on his knee. The image changed to a little girl, with blonde hair and blue eyes, squealing in delight as a Trevor presented her with a puppy peeking out of a red and green box. It brought another smile to my face. It was still there when I woke up the next morning.

THIRTY FIVE

RAPTOR

I WOKE UP AROUND seven o'clock in the morning, feeling lost without Adriana in my arms. I waited until nine, called her, and we made plans to meet after she was done working at Dazzle.

"I don't think I can wait that long to see you."

"I know," she said. "I missed you last night and this morning."

"Me, too. My penis is even having withdrawals, it missed you so much."

She laughed. "Withdrawals? Have you been playing with yourself?"

"Hell yeah. I've been looking at some pictures of you on my phone. I needed to do something to get rid of my woody."

"Oh, my God." She giggled. "Next time take a picture and send it to me."

"Of my cock?"

"Yes."

I grinned. My little sex kitten. "How about you spend the night and see it in person?"

"That sounds even better."

"I was hoping you'd say that. Pack an over-night bag."

"Okay."

"I love you."

"I love you, too."

After we hung up, I threw on a pair of jeans and a T-shirt, then stepped into the kitchen to make some coffee. As the coffee began to brew, I heard the doorbell. Not expecting anyone, and knowing that most of my friends called before showing up, I grabbed my gun and approached the door cautiously. When I saw who was waiting for me on the other side, I was in shock.

"Hello, Trevor," said my mother in a gravelly voice. She was smoking a cigarette and I could tell that both of her hands were shaking.

"Hi," I said, hiding the gun behind my shirt. I hadn't seen Mavis in almost fifteen years, and they'd been rough on her. From what I remembered, she was only in her fifties, but the lines on her face made her look decades older. She was also so thin, almost to the point of looking anorexic.

"You look good," she said, smiling. Some of her teeth were missing.

Meth, I thought, not wanting to pity her but unable to help myself.

"Thanks," I said.

She let out a ragged sigh. "We need to talk."

"We do, huh?" *Why now?* I wanted to ask.

"Yes. It's important."

"Is it about my brother?"

Her eyes widened. "You know about him?"

"Slammer told me."

"Oh. I forgot that he knows. Have you met him?"

"Briefly."

"That's more than what I've had. He refuses to see me," she said sadly. "I don't even know what he looks like."

I stared at her hard. "Not being able to see the person you love hurts, doesn't it?"

Mavis looked at me and her eyes filled with tears. "I'm so sorry, Trevor."

I sighed. "Why are you here?"

"Can we talk inside?" she asked. "It's cold out here."

I wanted to tell her to get lost, but she was still my mother and there was a part of me that didn't want her to leave. Not until she at least told me why she'd abandoned me.

I opened the door wider and stepped out of her way. "Come on in. Put your cigarette out first, though."

She took another drag of the smoke and then put it out with the sole of her boot. Shoving the butt into the pocket of her black wool coat, she stepped inside and whistled. "You've done real well for yourself, Trevor. Real well.

"Thanks," I replied stiffly.

She noticed my tone and turned to look at me. Her lips trembled. "I was always proud of you. You were a good boy. A smart boy."

I didn't say anything.

She looked away. "I know you're angry, Trevor. I can even understand why."

She could understand why? Fuck. "Would you like some coffee?" I asked, walking up the steps.

"Sure. That would be nice."

"Well, come on then," I said, when she didn't make any move to follow me.

"Let me take off my boots first."

"I'd appreciate it."

Still wearing her coat, which looked like it had seen better days, she followed me up the stairs and into the kitchen.

"Cream or sugar?" I asked, as she sat down.

"Neither," replied Mavis. "Thank you."

I set her cup of coffee down in front of her and she picked it up, her hands shaking so much, she could barely hold it.

"What's going on with that?" I asked, nodding toward her trembling fingers. "You still using?"

"No. I haven't used for a long time."

"You drinking?"

"No, not anymore. Just non-alcoholic beer sometimes. But, this isn't because of alcohol. I've got Parkinson's Disease," she said, shoving her hands into her lap. "I was diagnosed about a year ago."

I had a hard time believing her. "Is that right?"

"You don't have to believe me if you don't want to and I didn't come to ask you for sympathy."

"But, you came for something."

"Yes, I need –"

I interrupted her. "Money?"

"No, I need to tell you something," she said firmly. "Something that I overheard."

"What did you overhear?"

"The Devil's Rangers… they've ordered a hit on you and your brother."

"How did you find this out?" I asked, not surprised.

"I overheard two bikers talking about it, outside of Sal's. They didn't even know I was there, they were so drunk."

I scratched my chin. "They mention how much?"

"I didn't hear."

"Thanks for letting me know about it," I said, yawning.

"What are you going to do?" she asked, looking a little surprised at my lack of concern.

I took the gun out from behind my jeans and held it up. "Carry this around, I guess," I said and then set it down next to me.

She frowned. "You should do more than that. They want you badly. You killed the president of their chapter and his second in command."

"I didn't kill him," I answered, leaning against the counter with my coffee cup.

Mavis cocked her eyebrow. "It was Jordan, wasn't it?"

"I wasn't there. I have no clue who killed them," I lied. "As far as I'm concerned, they deserved what they got for the shit they've pulled."

She regarded me shrewdly. "Yes, you do know who killed them. I can see it in your eyes." Mavis smiled. "You never were particularly good at lying, Trevor."

I raised the cup to my lips and took a drink. "I guess I didn't get that trait from you."

Her lips pursed. "I did not lie to you. Yes, I left, but I never lied."

She may not have lied but she'd kept secrets. As far as I was concerned, it was the same thing. I laughed coldly at her logic. "Is that your big comeback? You abandoned me but you never lied about it? And that's supposed to be okay?"

She raised her hand. "No, you're right. It wasn't supposed to be 'okay', but I wasn't thinking clearly at the time. All I wanted was to escape your father's fists. Don't you remember our fights? He beat the hell out of me, Trevor. I was afraid that one day, he'd actually kill me. Can't you see why I had to get away?"

"*You* had to get away. What about me? I was still just a kid. I'm just lucky that Slammer took me in when he did."

She stared at me for a few seconds and then sighed. "I considered taking you with me, but then I knew that if I did, your father would have tracked me down. That's why I asked Slammer to watch over you."

"Bullshit, you just wanted to take the easy way out," I said, angrily.

"That's not it. I was frightened of taking you away from him. Your father didn't give a rat's ass about me. He told me that almost every day. But you? He loved you."

As far as I was concerned, he only loved himself and didn't give a shit about the boy he'd smacked around.

"Look, I didn't come here to argue," she said, looking weary. "I just wanted to let you know that they're after you." She stood up. "I'll get out of your hair now. Thanks for the coffee."

"Wait," I said, sighing. "Where are you staying?"

"I just moved in with a woman that I went to high school with. Berta Finnegan," she said, sitting back down.

"In Jensen?"

She nodded. "She lives in the trailer park over by St. Peters."

Near Misty's trailer, which was now abandoned. After the shit went down with Mud, she'd packed all of her bags and left town. Of course, Slammer had spooked the fuck out her with some outlandish threats. She'd believed him enough to get the hell out of Jensen, though. We hadn't heard from her since. "She work?"

Mavis smiled and nodded. "Yes. She's a Substance Abuse Counselor. She's been helping me with my drinking problem."

I raised my eyebrows. "How long have you been sober?"

"Four weeks now." Her smile fell. "I fucked up badly one night at Sal's, and knew it was time to get help. Fortunately, I'd been talking to Berta on Facebook and I reached out to her."

"What happened at Sal's?" I asked.

"I got really drunk and opened my mouth," she said, looking down at her hands. "I told someone about Jordan."

"What do you mean?" I asked.

"I was angry," she said, tears filling her eyes again. "Because he refused to see me. I got really drunk and talked about him to some of the regulars there."

"What did you say?"

"I said that he was my son. I also said some other stuff," she said, looking guilty. "That he wouldn't like."

"You gave up his identity," I said. "About him being the Judge?"

She nodded. "I know I fucked up but I was drunk and angry. When I realized what I did, the next day, I knew I had to do something about my drinking."

I sighed. "At least there's that."

She was silent for a few seconds. "I'm sure everyone knows who he is now. He's probably going to be pissed when he finds out who 'outed' him."

"I wouldn't worry too much about it," I said, seeing how scared she looked. "It's just Sal's."

"They have big mouths there. The entire town probably knows about it."

"I haven't heard anything, so obviously they don't."

"He's going to kill me, isn't he?"

"No, he's not going to kill you."

"He's already angry with me for leaving him with Acid. I had no choice there. You thought your father was bad?" She reached down and pulled up the leg of her jeans, exposing her calf. Just like Jordan's hand, her skin was scarred so badly, that I knew right away what it was.

"He used acid on you, too?"

She nodded and rolled her jeans back down. "He was evil, in every sense of the word. He used to handcuff me to the bed and torture me. I have more scars, but they're in places a son shouldn't see on his mother."

"Why didn't you call the cops?"

"I was so frightened of that man that I didn't think the cops could stop him. Hell, he used to play poker with a couple of them on Friday nights."

I pictured a young and frightened Mavis, feeling overwhelmed with fear. I couldn't blame her for wanting to escape such horror. I just wondered how she could have abandoned two of her children without fighting harder for them. Especially when she had friends like Slammer.

"I know what you're thinking," she said, staring at me. "But, I was very young and naïve and he was larger than life. In the end, he kicked me out and wouldn't allow me to see Jordan."

"And you never tried to see him?"

She shook her head. "No and I'm sure that's why he hates me so much."

"I don't think he hates you."

Mavis's eyes widened. "Why? Did he tell you that?"

"No, but he grew up with Acid and knew what kind of a monster he was. From what I see, he just has trust issues" I shrugged and looked away. "But, don't we all?"

"It's my fault. I know. I wish there was something I could do about it, now that my head is finally getting clear. But, I dug my own grave and believe it or not, I feel worthy of it."

My cell phone began to vibrate.

"I should go," she said, watching me grab it.

Nodding, I checked my phone and noticed that I'd received a call from a number that I didn't recognize.

Mavis picked up her satchel and turned toward the kitchen door. "I'll see you around."

"Let me walk you to the door," I said, following her out of the kitchen. When we reached the entryway, she slipped her boots back on and then turned to me.

"Take care of yourself," she said. "And don't forget to look out for those fucking Devil's Rangers."

"I will."

"If you know how to get ahold of Jordan, tell him the same thing. Also," her lip trembled again. "Tell him... that I'm sorry for everything. If I could go back and do things differently, I would." She reached up and touched my shoulder. "That goes for you, too."

Staring down at my mother, I wanted to forget the past and move forward. To hug the woman who had taught me how to tie my shoes and make pancakes. The woman who had once told me that she loved me more than life before abandoning me the morning after. I could see the sincerity in her eyes and I wanted things to be okay between us. But, I wasn't about to start singing, Kumbaya. "I'll let him know," I said, taking a step back from her.

Her face fell and I could tell she was disappointed. "Okay," she said, opening up the door. She turned around. "Do you have plans for Christmas?"

"Yes."

"Of course you do," she said and laughed nervously. "I'm not even sure why I asked. It was stupid of me. Well, Merry Christmas."

"Thanks. You, too," I answered.

With one last look, she walked down the porch and toward an old, blue Ford Taurus that was parked in front of the house. I watched as she got in, started it, and drove off. Brushing off an unexpected feeling of guilt, I checked my phone, to see if the person who'd called me had left a message. When I didn't see anything, I made myself some breakfast and then went downstairs to work out with my free weights. Afterward, I took a shower and headed out to the clubhouse.

THIRTY SIX

ADRIANA

AFTER TALKING WITH Trevor the next morning, I fell back asleep and slept until I heard my mother knock on my bedroom door.

"Yeah?" I mumbled, opening my eyes.

She opened the door and stared at me in surprise. "You're still sleeping? It's eleven, sleepy-head."

Yawning, I got out of bed. "It's the jet-lag," I said, scratching my shoulder. "I'm still wiped out."

"I bet. Well, come downstairs and I'll fix you some lunch," she answered. "That will help wake you up."

"Thanks. What time do you want me at Dazzle again?"

"Four?"

"Okay."

Mom left the room and as I stepped into my bathroom, I swore under my breath when I realized that I'd left the empty pregnancy test box out in the open. I buried it in the garbage can and then went downstairs to the kitchen.

"What are you hungry for?" my mother asked, looking into the refrigerator.

"Just something easy," I replied, sitting at the counter.

She turned and looked at me. "How about some macaroni-and-cheese? I can make you my special recipe."

"The homemade kind? That would be great," I said, turning on the television. She made the best macaroni-and-cheese, even making her own noodles from scratch. "Are you sure you have time?"

She pulled out a bag of flour from the cupboard. "Enough time

241

to make you your favorite. We haven't had a lot of time together, lately, and I know how much you love this recipe."

"That's so sweet. Thanks, Mom," I said, looking at her. "Do you want any help?"

"No," she said laughing. The last time I'd tried helping her with it, I'd burned the noodles, which was apparently not an easy thing to do, especially when you boiled them. "Just let me do it."

"Okay," I replied, relieved.

"So, are you seeing Trevor later this evening?" she asked, walking back over to the refrigerator.

"Actually, yes. I'm staying over at his place tonight."

"It's probably good. There's supposed to be another snowstorm," she said, pulling out a carton of eggs and a gallon of milk. "Sometime after eleven. I hear we could even get between four and eight inches of snow."

"Great," I said dryly. "Tomorrow is going to be a mess on the roads and I need to get some Christmas shopping done."

"Just be careful driving."

"Do you want me to get home early in the morning so I can help snow-blow the driveway?"

"Jim already promised to do it."

I grinned. "He sure is a nice guy."

She smiled back. "I know and very handy. When you were gone last week, he helped replace my water heater. Thank goodness he was here when it went out, otherwise I would have called someone else and spent a fortune."

"When did it go out?"

"Friday morning."

My eyes widened. "He was here last Friday morning?"

Her cheeks turned pink.

My jaw dropped. "He spent the night, didn't he?"

She took out a bowl from the cupboard, avoiding my eyes. "Yes."

"Did you guys… you know?"

She didn't say anything.

I grinned. "Mom, you did, didn't you?"

She sighed. "Yes, we did. Are you happy?"

"The question is, are you happy?"

I didn't think she was going to answer, but then she suddenly smiled and nodded. "It was nice."

"Nice?"

Her eyes widened. "Yes, nice, and that's all I'm going to say about it. It was very nice and we both enjoyed ourselves."

I laughed. "Okay. That's good to know."

She started mixing her ingredients for the noodles and a small smile crept onto her lips.

"What are you smiling about?"

She looked at me. "I'm just… happy."

"Happy? You mean you're in love, aren't you?"

Vanda's eyes sparkled. "Yes. I believe I am."

"That's great," I said, excited for her. "What about Jim? Does he love you?"

"Yes. He admitted it to me a couple of weeks ago."

"That's fabulous!" I said, surprised that she hadn't mentioned it yet. "So, when's the wedding?"

"Wedding?"

"Yeah. Aren't you two going to get married?" I teased.

"No. Of course not"

"What do you mean?" I said, feeling excited for her. "Why not? Has he asked you?"

She smiled. "He did, as a matter of fact."

"Then why not? You don't have to have a big wedding. You could elope in Maui, like Slammer and Frannie did. Or, pick another island or a totally different location. Even Vegas!"

She looked at me and chuckled. "It's a beautiful thought, but we aren't getting married."

"Maybe you'll change your mind after you think about it for a while?"

She didn't answer. Instead, she began rolling out the dough for the noodles. "You're in a great mood today," she said, changing the subject. "You *must* have slept well."

That and I'd had a wonderful dream about Trevor and me at a beach, playing in the sand with our baby. I couldn't tell if it was a boy or a girl, but we were having fun and I hadn't wanted the dream to end. "I'm still tired but I feel pretty good."

"Good."

The house phone rang and I got up to answer it.

"May I please speak to Vanda Nikolas?" asked a man on the other end.

"Sure." I held the phone up. "Mom, it's for you."

"I'll be right there," she said, rushing over to the sink to wash her hands. When she was finished, Vanda grabbed the phone and walked away with it.

As they talked, I started flipping through the channels but then stopped when I recognized the photograph of a woman on the news.

It was April!

"Oh, my God," I said, stunned at the news of her being 'Wanted' for questioning by the police. As I listened to the journalist, I learned that April's brother had been found murdered in Hayward, Minnesota.

"Okay. I'll see you next week," murmured Vanda. "Goodbye."

Not paying much attention to my mother, I started thinking back to the night April had helped us escape Mud and Skull. She hadn't seemed like a particularly violent woman, but I began to wonder if she'd killed her brother. Then when I heard that the murder had occurred a few days after we'd left Hayward, I knew it wasn't her. I wondered if the Devil's Rangers had anything to do with it and decided to call Trevor.

"I'll be right back," I said, flipping off the television.

"Where are you going?" she asked, looking a little troubled.

"Just to use my phone. Are you okay?"

"I'm fine."

"Who was that on the phone?"

Vanda took a little long to answer. "Nobody important. I'm going to start cooking the noodles and getting the cheese melted. The food should be ready soon."

"Okay," I answered, leaving the kitchen. I ran upstairs and grabbed my phone.

"Kitten, is everything okay?" asked Trevor, when I called him.

"I don't know, you tell me," I said and then explained what I'd seen on the news.

"It might be nothing but then again, it could be them," said Trevor, sounding a little worried himself.

"The Devil's Rangers?"

"Yes."

I let out a ragged breath. "Are they going to come looking for me?"

"They might try and that's why I want you to move in with me. Now, instead of later. I don't want to give them another chance to snatch you from your home, like they did last time."

"Yeah, but they snatched Brandy from your home," I protested. "What makes you think that they won't go looking for me there as well?"

"I won't let you out of my sight," he said. "If they show up, they'll meet me *and* their maker."

I smiled at his words. "That won't work. You can't watch over me every second of the day and I have school. You can't follow me to my classes."

He was silent.

"Trevor?"

"Okay, fine. I'll hire a bodyguard to watch over you when I'm not able to."

"I can't live like that. Being followed all the time. I'll feel foolish."

"Better to feel something than get killed."

I gasped. "Do you really think they're planning on killing me?"

"I think they're looking for revenge and coming after us is the only way they'll get it."

"What about that guy? The one who killed Skull? Can he help us?"

"We don't need his help, Kitten. I just need you to move in here with me. I'll put in a security system and you can learn how to use a gun."

"I already know how to use a gun," I said, feeling frustrated. "But, the hell if I really want to carry one around. I don't even have a Carry-and-Conceal permit." I doubted he had one either, but this was me and I wasn't interested in taking chances. Not when it came to the law and handguns.

"Then let me find someone to watch over you when I can't."

I touched my stomach, wondering what I'd gotten myself into. I loved Trevor with all of my heart, but now I was bringing another life into the world and its life was already in danger. "Why does this stuff keep happening? Can't you just call your other Chapters and come down on these guys all together?"

"Actually, I think Slammer is heading in that direction."

"God, I hope so."

"Until then, you're moving in," he said firmly.

"What about my mother? Will she be in danger?"

"I think she'll be fine."

"I don't know. Look at what happened to April's brother," I protested. "If anything happens to her I'd never be able to live with myself."

"We don't know if April's brother's death was even related to the Devil's Rangers. It's just speculation."

"I wish I knew how to get ahold of her," I said, chewing on my lip. "Then we'd know for sure."

My mother knocked on the door and then stuck her head into my room. "Your food is done."

"Okay," I said, trying to sound more chipper than how I felt. "I'll be right down."

Nodding, she left.

"I have to go and eat lunch," I told him.

"Okay. Remember, I'm going to meet you at Dazzle tonight. We'll talk to your mother together. About you moving in."

"She's going to freak out, you know. This is so much to lay on her." Too much.

"We don't have any other choice. She needs to know the truth. It's for her safety, too."

"I know."

"Did you tell her about the baby yet?"

"No. I wanted to wait until after the holidays."

"How are you handling it today? Better than yesterday?"

"I was feeling much better until I saw the news," I mumbled. "What about you?"

"I'm stoked about the baby. I could barely sleep."

"Stoked?" I replied, picturing his smiling face.

"Yes and not just about our child. I'm happy about us getting married and living together. Aren't you excited?"

"Yes," I replied with not quite as much enthusiasm. "I am."

He sighed. "Relax and don't let this shit worry you, Kitten. I'll keep you safe, this time. I promise."

I know you'll at least give it your best shot.

THIRTY SEVEN

RAPTOR

"**H**OW'D SHE FIND out?" asked Tank after I hung up with Adriana. It was just after twelve and he'd asked if I wanted to drive out to Prairie Lake to do some snowmobiling before our meeting at three. He owned two Polaris Indy Eight-hundreds and the weather was now perfect for sledding, especially with the fresh snow.

I grabbed my leather jacket and pulled it on. "The morning news."

"Oh. I was hoping she'd miss it."

"Me, too."

Tank put his gloves on and flexed his hands. He was wearing a snowmobile jacket, bibs, and Sorel winter boots. "You ready to go and have some fun?"

"Hell yeah," I said, now following him out the front door of the clubhouse. "Although, I'm not really dressed for it."

He shrugged. "I've got an extra jacket, if your leather isn't warm enough."

"As long as you have a helmet, I'm good," I answered.

"Suit yourself."

As we walked toward his trailer, I could tell that the wind had picked up. I decided to take him up on the offer of the jacket when we got to the lake.

"Guess who shocked the fuck out of me this morning?" I said as we drove away.

"Who?"

"My mother."

"No shit? Mavis? What did she want?"

"She came to warn me about the Devil's Rangers. Apparently, they've ordered a hit on my head. Mine and The Judge's."

Tank laughed. "Really?"

"Maybe I should warn him," I said, now smiling myself.

"It might solve all of our problems," said Tank. "Especially if he takes out their entire Chapter. If anyone can do it without breaking a sweat, it's him."

I nodded and pulled out my phone.

"What are you doing?" asked Tank.

"I'm going to send him a text. To let him know," I said, typing.

"Good idea. I can't wait to see his response."

I'd never sent Jordan a text message before, but I didn't feel like disturbing him with a phone call, especially in his line of work.

The lake was deserted when we arrived, which wasn't any surprise, considering the fact that it was a Tuesday and most people were at work. After we unloaded the sleds and started them up, Tank threw me his other Colombia jacket.

"Thanks," I said, removing my leather. "It's colder than I thought."

"It's only about twenty-five degrees," he said. "No sense in freezing your ass off."

Agreeing, I zipped up the jacket and grabbed a helmet. "Where do you want to ride?"

"Just around the lake," he said, locking up the truck after I shoved my leather inside the cab. "Let's go riding, brother."

We jumped onto the sleds and it only took me a few seconds to get acclimated to mine. After a while, we began racing toward the other end of the lake, both of us trying outride each other. Eventually,

I pulled ahead, being the smaller driver, and we turned around and went back the same way. We spent the next hour-and-a-half exploring the lake, chasing each other, and laughing our asses off. When it was time to load the sleds back onto the trailer and head back to the clubhouse, neither of us could stop grinning. The winters in Jensen were long and I was already missing my bike, but being on that sled had felt real fucking good.

"I needed that. Thanks for inviting me," I told him.

"No problem, brother. We *both* needed that. It was a good time."

"It was," I said as we strapped the sleds back onto the trailer. "Next time we should hit the trails up north."

"That's what I was thinking. Like last year. Make it an all-day run."

"Hell, yeah."

"You need to do as much as you can before that kid of yours comes into the world. Once Adriana pops it out, you won't have much spare time."

"Good point."

When the sleds were secure, I changed back into my leather jacket, and we hopped back into the truck. Hearing my cell phone go off, I pulled it out.

"Who is it?"

"The Judge left me a text," I said, checking the message.

"What did he say?"

I smiled. "You called it. He said he'd take care of it."

"I told you," said Tank, with a shit-eating grin. "What else did he say?"

"That's it."

"Huh."

I sent him another message, asking him that meant.

He called me.

"It means don't worry, I'm handling the situation," he said.

"Did you see the news report, about that guy in Hayward? The one that was murdered? It was April's brother."

"Who's April?" he asked.

I told him.

He was silent for a few seconds. "Where is she now?"

"We have no idea."

"You got a last name for her?"

"No."

"She mean anything to you?"

"Other than that she helped save my girl, not much. I'd just hate to see her murdered."

"Same with me," said Tank loudly. "The woman is too hot to die."

"I'll look into her brother's murder and see what I can find out. As far as the rest of those fuck-heads in Hayward, you'll be reading their obituaries in another week."

"I'm glad we're kin. I'd hate to have you on my enemy list."

"Acid was kin."

There it was. He'd just admitted to killing his old man.

"Speaking of kin, Mavis showed up on my doorstep this morning. She wanted me to tell you that she was sorry for being a lousy mother and abandoning the both of us. Acid scared the fuck out of her."

"I'm sure he did. I don't have any sympathy for her, though. She made her choices and most of them were selfish."

"I agree."

"I have to go. I'm in the middle of something."

"An assignment?"

"I'll let you know when the Hayward Chapter of the Devil's Rangers isn't a problem anymore," he said, ignoring my question.

"You sure you don't want to get together for Christmas?" I joked, waiting for a cocky comeback. Instead of delivering, he simply hung up.

I looked at Tank as I put my phone away. "I think I'm growing on him."

Tank grunted.

THIRTY EIGHT

ADRIANA

AFTER VANDA LEFT for work, I called my Gynecologist and made an appointment for the following week. I spoke to a nurse and told her that I thought I was pregnant.

"Did you take a home pregnancy test?" she asked.

"Yes. Two of them."

"What did the test results show?"

"That I was pregnant."

"Then you probably are. They're pretty accurate, especially if you get a positive test result. Okay, we'll see you next week, then?"

"Yes."

After hanging up, I took a shower and then grabbed a pair of black slacks and a green turtleneck sweater. The pants, which used to be loose-fitting, were hard to button and I made a mental note to go shopping for new ones while I was searching for gifts the following day. I then took out my suitcase and began filling it with clothes. Although I'd stayed at Trevor's place before, this time I was packing for a stay that would become permanent. I felt excited, and yet the thought of leaving my mother all alone made me anxious and a little sad. Trevor had said that she'd be fine, but I wasn't so sure. The only thing that comforted me was that she had Jim.

Maybe it would be the push she needed to marry the man?

He was certainly good to her and now both of them were in love. They deserved to be together and I hoped that she'd change her mind.

When I packed as much as I could into my suitcase, I grabbed a duffel bag and started stuffing my toiletries into it. When I'd gotten what I could into the bag, I looked around my bedroom, knowing that there were still quite a few things that I'd need to come back for. As I carried the luggage downstairs, my cell phone rang.

"How was your trip?" asked Tiffany, when I answered it.

"It was amazing," I smiled. "The best time of my life, actually." I told her about some of the excursions we had done.

"I'm so jealous. I haven't been on a trip in so long and I've always wanted to visit Hawaii. I wonder if I can talk Jeremy into going…"

"You two are still dating?" I asked, surprised.

"Yes."

"Wow."

"Yeah, I know. We finally had sex, too."

"Oh? And how was that?"

"Nice. Very nice. He certainly knows how to use his gun."

I laughed. "And he let you play with it? Isn't that dangerous?"

She laughed, too. "Probably. Maybe that's why he handcuffed me to the bed."

"Oh, my. I'm never going to look at Detective Stone the same way again."

"You and me both. Anyway, what are you doing for New Year's Eve?"

"I'm not sure. We haven't made any plans yet. What about you?"

"Jeremy is having a party and told me to invite you."

"Really? I'll have to talk it over with Trevor. Those two don't really get along, you know?"

"They can get over themselves and push aside their differences for a few hours. Anyway, I have to get back to work. I'm on my lunch break."

"Well, thanks for inviting us. I'll talk to him and find out if he's already made plans. I have a feeling that he celebrates New Years with his biker friends."

"You're probably right. Maybe you can just stop in for a drink?"

I wanted to tell her that I couldn't have alcohol, not while I was pregnant, but I just couldn't get myself to bring it up. I wanted my mother to hear about it before my friends.

"Maybe," I said. "I'll call you."

"Sounds good."

After we hung up, I packed my stuff into the trunk of my car and headed out to Dazzle early. When I arrived, they were busy with customers.

"Hi there," said Jim, who was at his usual post, which was near the door. Tim was also in the shop, helping a customer at one of the counters. Other than that, the place looked pretty bare.

"Hi, Jim," I said, smiling at him.

He folded his newspaper and set it down. "How was your trip?"

"We had so much fun. With this crappy weather we're having, I wish I was back there. Have you ever been to Hawaii?"

"No, but I'd love to take a trip there some day."

"You and my mother should go," I said, lowering my voice. "You'd have so much fun. I know she'd love it."

He winked. "I was thinking the same thing."

Winking back, I headed toward the back of the store.

"Hi, Mom," I said, as she walked out of the break room.

"Oh, you're here early," she answered. "Good, we can use the help."

"Are you okay?" I asked, noticing that she was pasty looking.

She waved her hand. "Don't worry about me, I'm fine."

"You don't look fine. Why don't you go back and relax?" I said, worried about her.

"I was just doing that," she said. "Like I said, don't worry about me. I'm just a little tired."

"Do you want me to go and buy you one of those lattes that you like so much? From the coffee shop?"

"Maybe later."

"Okay," I said, still unsure. "I'll go put my jacket in back."

"Thanks for coming in early, by the way. Gerald is at lunch right now and I have a feeling we're going to get hit any minute with a slew of customers."

"Yeah, I'm sure. I'll be back in a second," I replied, heading toward the back room.

"Nice tan," said Tim, looking at me over his shoulder when I returned. "With this weather, you must miss being back in Maui."

"It was beautiful," I admitted. "Have you been there before?"

"Yes. I love it. I'm trying to talk Juan into going. He's afraid of flying, though."

"They have prescriptions for that," said Tim's customer, a middle-aged man who was looking at bracelets. "Sedatives. My wife hates flying, too. If it wasn't for the pills, she'd never get on a plane."

"That's good to know," said Tim. "We'll have to look into it. I need a vacation."

"To tell you the truth, I was a little nervous during our flight," I said, chuckling. "I could have used something myself."

"Vanda, are you okay?" asked Tim, staring over my head.

I turned to look at my mother, who was now standing next to the register and swaying slightly. I frowned. "Mom, what's wrong?"

"I… I don't feel well," she said in a breathy voice.

"Maybe you should sit down," I told her.

Instead of answering, her eyes rolled to the back of her head and she fainted.

"Oh, my God!" I cried, dropping down to my knees next to her. "Mom!?"

Jim rushed over. "Vanda," he said, kneeling down. He felt for a pulse and looked at me, his eyes wide with fear. "We'd better call an ambulance."

THIRTY NINE

RAPTOR

WHEN WE ARRIVED back at the clubhouse, Slammer was sitting at the bar talking to someone I didn't recognize.

"Who's that?" I said to Tank, noticing the familiar patches. "Talking to your old man?"

"Jesus. I think that's Bastard."

"He doesn't look too happy."

"No, he doesn't."

Bastard had founded the Gold Vipers and was still running the Mother Chapter in Sacramento. I'd never met him but had heard that he was a pretty fair guy.

Tank and I walked over and introduced ourselves.

"So, you're Raptor," said Bastard, shaking my hand. "Shit's been piling up for you lately, hasn't it?"

I shrugged. "Nothing I can't handle."

"That's what I've also heard. Doesn't hurt to have a man like The Judge watching your back, either."

"I don't know if he's watching my back, but he's certainly been a big help."

"Just be glad he's on your side."

"Oh, I am. Believe me."

Bastard turned to Slammer. "I've got to head out. I just wanted to stop by and let you know we're stepping in now too. This shit has gone too far."

"I appreciate that. We all do," said Slammer.

"April," called Bastard. "We're heading out."

Tank and I turned to see the familiar blonde who had driven Adriana and Brandy away from Mud's clubhouse, on the night they'd been kidnapped. She walked over to Bastard and snuggled up to him.

"Long time no see," she said, winking at us.

We just stared at her, stunned.

"Like to introduce you to my new Old Lady," said Bastard, who was old enough to be her grandfather. "But I've heard that you've already met."

"The question is, how did you two meet?" asked Tank, now chuckling.

"At a biker bar," said April. "After I left Minnesota, I drove out to California and stayed with a girlfriend, I hadn't seen in years. She dragged me to this bar in Sacramento a couple of days ago, and we clicked right off the bat."

"Two days, huh?" said Slammer. "And he's claimed you already?"

"It was love at first sight for me," said Bastard, squeezing one of her breasts. "And when you get to be my age, you don't let go of something this beautiful when it falls into your lap. I patched her last night so we could make it official."

She slapped his hand playfully. "I think you patched me so you can keep playing with my boobs," she said, smiling. "Anyway, I couldn't believe the coincidence when I found out that he was in the same biker club that Mud had declared war on. I mean, what are the chances of that?"

"It was meant to be," said Bastard, winking at me.

I wasn't sure who she was trying to kid, but it was obvious that April had set her sights on Bastard for her own cause. He knew it. We knew it. But, nobody cared. Bastard wasn't getting any younger and April was definitely one hot chick. It was a win-win situation for the both of them.

"What about your brother?" asked Tank. "We heard what happened."

Her smile fell. "Bastard said he'd make sure they get what's coming to them."

"They will, April," he said, pulling her close. "It's already being handled."

"It is?" I asked, wondering if he'd also been in contact with The Judge.

"Yeah. We're just taking a trip up there to make sure nothing gets missed. April and I just wanted to stop by to let you know. Especially you, Raptor. Heard there's a hit on you. I don't think you're going to have to worry about it anymore."

"Good to hear," I said.

"We'd better go," said Bastard, looking tired. "We have a three hour trip and I'm already bushed."

"Don't worry, I'm driving," said April.

"I was hoping you'd say that," he replied.

"Tell Adriana I said 'hi'," said April. "She's an awesome chick. I'm hoping that we can get together and shoot the shit again one day. Under better circumstances than last time, of course."

"I will. Thanks again, April. You helped them escape. If it wasn't for you, Mud might have gotten to her before he was taken out. I owe you," I said.

She looked at Bastard and then winked at me. "Owe me? Nah, I think we're all good."

I smiled.

FORTY

ADRIANA

Y MOTHER REGAINED consciousness right before the ambulance arrived.

"Why did you call them?" she asked, looking embarrassed as she brushed off her dress and stood back up. "I'm fine. I'm just a little weak. Call them back and tell them to forget it."

"No," said Jim firmly. "You fainted and someone needs to check you out."

"It's my own fault," she said, forcing a smile to her face. "I haven't been eating or sleeping much. I'll work on it."

"No, it's more than that," said Jim. He looked at me and then back to her. "You need to see a doctor. You've been complaining about severe headaches and pressure... now this?"

"You've been having headaches?" I asked. "Why haven't you seen a doctor?"

"I saw one," she said, lowering her voice. "Last week."

"What did they say?" Jim and I asked in unison.

"Not a lot. Anyway, we'll talk about it later," she answered. "Just don't worry about me. I'm fine. I just need something to drink."

"What would you like?" I asked.

"An orange juice would be good," she answered and smiled. "Thank you."

"What about food?" I asked. "You said you haven't been eating right."

"A sandwich sounds good," she replied. "I'm sorry. I feel so stupid."

"You're not stupid," I said firmly. "But you should take better care of yourself."

"She's right," said Jim. "From now on, I'm going to make sure

267

you get enough nutrients in your body, even if I had to hand-feed you myself."

Just then, two paramedics walked through the front door of the shop.

"Over here," said Jim, flagging them toward us.

"What's going on?" asked one of them, a short, stocky man with black hair and glasses.

"She fainted," said Jim, pointing to Vanda.

"I'm fine now, though," she said, looking embarrassed again. "You don't have to waste your time here. Go and help someone who really needs it."

"You should still let them look at you," said Tim, also looking concerned.

"What happened?" asked the man, whose nametag read "Phil."

Vanda tried explaining that she'd fainted because she hadn't been eating right or sleeping enough. When she was finished, the other paramedic, a woman named Bonnie, offered to assess her vital signs.

"It's better to be safe than sorry," said Bonnie. "Sometimes, you think you know… but you really don't."

"Exactly," said Tim, walking back toward his customer. "We don't want anything happening to you, Vanda. Let them check you out."

"Fine," she said, looking defeated. She turned to me. "Could you stay inside and watch the store? I'll be right back."

"Of course."

"I'll go with them," said Jim, as the two paramedics led Vanda away. "She's so stubborn that even if something was wrong, she wouldn't tell us."

"I know. Thanks."

While they were outside, two other customers walked into the store and I managed to sell one of them an expensive ruby ring, even though my mind was on my mother the entire time I was presenting it. The fact that she'd been having headaches and had gone as far as to see a doctor about them, worried me.

"Your wife is going to love the ring," I told the man after wrapping it up for him in Christmas paper and decorating it with a bow. "And... thanks so much for your business. We really do appreciate it."

"You're welcome," he said, just as my mother and Jim walked back into the shop. "Enjoy your Christmas."

"You, too."

"Merry Christmas," said Vanda, as the customer walked by her.

"You, too, Vanda. Take care of yourself," he replied.

"I will. Thank you."

"What did they say?" I asked when she approached the register.

"Just like I said, I'm fine. I just need to eat better and rest more."

"Okay, well that's good news," I replied. "I'll go and get you that sandwich you wanted."

"And the orange juice," she said.

I smiled. "Of course."

"I'm going to go and sit down in back," she said and then turned to Jim. "If we get too busy, call me on the intercom. Gerald should be back soon, but it will just be Tim on the floor until then."

"You just go back and put your feet up," he scolded. "And let me worry about the customers."

"Fine," she huffed. "But, like I said –"

"Mom, the store will be fine. Go in back and relax. I'll be back in a jiffy."

"You two. What would I do without you?" she said, her eyes growing misty.

I kissed her on the cheek. "What would we do without you? Now, go and do what Jim said. He has a gun. I wouldn't piss him off."

"Fine," she replied, smiling at him.

I grabbed my purse and jacket, then drove to a small deli that I knew my mother frequented. After purchasing a turkey sandwich and a bottle of orange juice, I drove back to the shop, all the while re-thinking my plans to move out of her house. After watching Vanda faint, I didn't know if I had it in me to leave her alone in the house.

"Here you go," I said, handing her the bag of food. She was in her office and on her computer.

"Thanks. Just set it there," she said, pointing.

"What are you doing?" I asked, setting it down on her desk.

"Just checking on the company finances."

"Oh."

"Tell me the truth," she said, opening up the bag of food. "When I'm gone, would you be happy running this shop?"

My eyes widened. "I don't know. Why are you bringing this up?"

"I won't be around forever and I'm just curious as to what you'd like to do with the company? Run it? Sell it?"

"You're really making me nervous with all of this talk about death," I replied.

"I know, but it's a part of life, Adriana." She unwrapped the sandwich. "Oh, this looks so good. Thank you."

"You're welcome."

"The fact is that I'm no spring chicken," said Vanda, looking back at me. "And that's why I need to start thinking about the future of this company. Are you interested in running it?"

"I guess so," I replied. "I mean, it's why I'm taking the classes that I am."

She nodded and smiled. "Good. I just wanted to know for sure."

"I'd better get back out there. By the way, Gerald is back," I told her.

"I know."

I stared at her, still uneasy. "Mom, I'm worried about you. Are you sure you're not holding something back from me?"

"No, don't be silly. I just need to take better care of myself. That's all. You just worry about yourself, okay?"

"Fine," I replied. "And you'd better. You gave us all quite a scare when you fainted."

"I know. I'm sorry. See, I'm eating," she said and took a bite of her sandwich.

Satisfied, I turned and left her office.

FORTY ONE

ADRIANA

THE REST OF the day flew by because we were so busy. Around six, my mother ordered pizza, under Jim's orders, and each of us took breaks to eat when time allowed.

"Trevor is here," informed my mother, around nine-thirty. I'd just finished with a customer and was in the back, nibbling on the last few slices of pizza.

"Oh. Okay," I replied, wiping my mouth

"At least one of us has a big appetite," she said, smiling.

"I'm definitely not lacking there," I replied, turning the sink on to wash my hands.

"He's looking at rings."

I turned to look at her. "Oh yeah?"

She nodded.

I grinned.

Vanda looked uneasy. "Things are getting serious between you?"

I turned off the water and grabbed a paper towel. "Yes, Mom. I told you before – we're in love."

"Love. You barely know each other."

I dried my hands. "I don't know about that. We've been spending a lot of time together. I think we know each other pretty well, especially after Hawaii. He's a good man, despite what you think of him. You just need to get to know Trevor better."

She didn't reply.

I walked around her and stepped into the shop, happy that my shift was almost over. When I spotted him, he was looking at engagement rings with Tim. He had on the leather jacket his grandmother had given him, and his hair was pulled into a ponytail.

"Hi," I said, approaching them.

Trevor gave me one of his sexy smiles and the light blue shirt he wore under his jacket made his eyes pop. "Hello, beautiful. Am I glad to see you…"

"Bad day" I asked, as Tim smiled at me and quietly walked away.

"Not really. I just missed you," he said, leaning forward to kiss me.

"I missed you, too," I said, when we pulled away.

"Hello, Trevor," said my mother, approaching us.

"Hello," he said, his expression more guarded.

"You look very nice," she replied, smiling at him with real warmth this time.

He grinned. "Well, thank you, Vanda." He looked down at his jacket. "Glad you approve."

"You clean up nice. Tell me, did you ride your motorcycle tonight?"

He laughed. "No. Believe it or not, I have a truck. I'd prefer the bike, but it doesn't travel well this time of the year."

"No, I'm sure it doesn't." She looked down at the rings under the glass. "Are you shopping for something? Or just waiting for Adriana?"

Without answering directly, he looked down and pointed at one of the diamond rings – a one-and-a-half carat princess-cut solitaire. "I was looking at that. It's gorgeous," he said and then looked at me. "Do you like it?"

I knew that particular ring was over twelve grand. "It's beautiful, but—"

"But, nothing," said Vanda. "I thought I trained you better, Adriana.

Never say something like that to a potential customer. Would you like to see the ring?"

"Sure," he replied, winking at me.

Vanda opened up the case and took the ring out. She held it up to the light. "This one is almost completely flawless and do you see the color? There is none. It's very rare."

"It's also very expensive," I said. "There are others that are also beautiful and you don't have to take out a second mortgage to make a purchase."

"We have financing," said Vanda, smiling. "If you'd like to see if you qualify?"

"I can't see why I wouldn't. My credit is kick ass," he said. "Try it on, Kitten."

Mom turned to me, her eyebrow raise. "Kitten?"

"Pet name, obviously," I said, wishing she'd go away.

"I see. Why don't you try it on, *Kitten*?" she asked with a smile.

I'd already tried it on before. Many times. It was the nicest one we carried, outside of the vault. The pricier rings weren't even in the showroom. This particular diamond was gorgeous but as far as I was concerned, not necessary. Even with a family discount, it would still be thousands of dollars.

"No, that's okay," I said.

"Oh for Heaven's sake, try it on. You know you want to," she said, handing it to me.

"Fine," I said, taking it. I slid it over my finger and noticed that it was very snug.

"No problem. We can always get it resized," said Vanda. "Or, you can cut back on your sodium intake."

I grunted. "Thanks, Mom."

"I think the ring is beautiful," said Trevor, examining the ring on my finger. Our eyes met. "Do you like it?"

"Of course I do," I said. "But, it's too expensive."

"I'll be the judge of that," he said. "How much is it, anyway?"

She told him and he didn't even flinch.

"I figured it was something like that. How many carats?"

"One-and-a-half."

"Is that big enough?" he asked. "Maybe we should look at two carats."

I laughed nervously, wondering what he was thinking. We hadn't even told my mother about moving in together, and here he was looking at engagement rings with her. It felt a little surreal. "No, I don't think we need to look at two carats. This one is more than I need anyway."

He smiled. "You're worth every penny."

"She is," said my mother as I handed her back the ring. "So, is there something that you two wanted to tell me?"

Trevor and I looked at each other and then he cleared his throat.

"Actually, yes. We're thinking about getting married," he said.

"Thinking about getting married," she repeated. "I'd say that if you're looking at engagement rings, you've been thinking about it pretty hard."

"We both have," I said, grateful that there were only a couple of other customers in the store and they weren't nearby. I didn't want anyone to hear the lecture that I knew was coming.

"Why do you want to marry my daughter?" she asked him.

"Because I love Adriana with all my heart and couldn't imagine living my life without her," he said softly.

My eyes misted up and I smiled at him.

Mom looked at me, her expression unreadable. "And why do you want to marry Trevor?"

"Because I feel the same way. We're in love."

"You're so young," she said, now looking at me sadly. "Can't you wait?"

"We could, but why?" I asked.

"You have so much living to do," she replied. "And then there's school. Don't jump into something you might not be ready for."

"Mom, didn't you tell me that your parents tried talking you out of getting married, because they didn't think you were ready?"

"I was older and they were wrong. I was ready."

"I'm ready, too."

She looked at Trevor, who'd been quiet. "And what do you have to say about all of this?"

"I'm willing to wait until she's ready. It's totally up to her. I just want her in my life and I'm willing to do whatever it takes to make her happy."

"Even marriage?" asked Vanda.

"Especially marriage."

She took a deep breath and exhaled. "I see. Well, you're both adults and I know you're going to do what you want."

"We'd like your blessing, though," said Trevor.

She nodded slowly. "If you promise to honor, love, and protect my daughter, I will give that to you."

"Really?" I squealed, shocked that she'd relented so easily.

"I promise, Vanda. I will. Thank you," he replied, just as surprised as me.

"I want you to know, though," she said, her eyes narrow, "if you hurt her or she gets involved in something illegal, because of your gang or lifestyle, I will hunt you down and shoot you myself."

"I understand," he said, smiling. "And I take your threat very seriously. She's safe with me."

"She'd better be," said Vanda, her shoulders relaxing. She smiled. "Now, do you like that ring? I know the owner of this joint and I think if we play our cards right, we can talk her down in price."

Trevor and I both laughed.

FORTY TWO

ADRIANA

A LTHOUGH MY MOTHER took the news of us getting married surprisingly well, we didn't tell her about the pregnancy. I didn't want her to think that we were getting married just because I was pregnant, especially after the talk we had with her in the shop.

"We forgot to tell her that you were moving in with me, too," he said afterward, when we were getting into our vehicles.

"About that," I said. "I think we should wait a few weeks."

"Why?"

I told him how she'd fainted in the shop. "She said she'd seen a doctor, too, about her headaches."

"What did the doctor say?"

"I'm not sure. She brushed it off."

He sighed. "You're going to stay the night though, right?"

"Of course," I said. "We'll break the news of us moving in together on Christmas Eve. She's making dinner. You're invited, by the way. Unless, you have other plans?"

"This year, my plans are with you," he said, pulling me into his arms.

"What about your grandmother?" I still hadn't met her yet. All I knew was that she lived in Florida with her "Old Man" and that they traveled a lot on their bikes.

"She's on a cruise right now," he said. "But, I spoke to her about two weeks ago and told her about you. She wants us to visit her soon. Maybe after the holidays?"

"Sure. I'd love to meet her. That's your mom's mother, right?"

"Yeah." He told me about his mother showing up at his doorstep,

281

earlier in the day.

"What did she want?"

He went over their conversation. When he got to the part about the Devil's Rangers, I gasped in horror. "There's a 'hit' on you?"

"From what I hear, it's been canceled," he said, smirking.

"Canceled?"

He told me about Bastard and April.

"Do you think she sought him out on purpose?" I asked, surprised.

"Oh yeah," he replied, smiling. "But, he knows and doesn't seem to care."

"I guess that worked out in everyone's favor then," I replied, relieved that the Mother Chapter was finally stepping in. "Does that mean we don't have to worry about the Devil's Rangers anymore?"

"For the time being. At least that Chapter."

"They have a Mother Chapter, too, don't they?" I replied.

"Yes."

"What will they do?"

"I don't know."

"Could they retaliate?"

"Probably."

"This is nuts," I said, frustrated. "I feel like there is always going to be some kind of threat for us."

"Don't think that way. It's not going to be like that. We're going to get married, have this baby, and live to see our grandkids do the same thing. Hell, I shouldn't have opened my big mouth. The Devil's Rangers aren't worth stressing over."

I knew that he was saying it so I wouldn't worry, but I wasn't naïve. Our lives were still in danger and it would always be the case, as long as long as there were Devil's Rangers.

"I promised your mother that I'd protect you, and I will," he said, pulling me back into his arms. "Just don't ever shut me out, Kitten."

"I won't, Trevor." I closed my eyes and let him hold me. As worried as I was, I loved him and would never walk away. This was now my life and there really was no turning back.

FORTY THREE

ADRIANA

TREVOR SHOWED UP on Christmas Eve with a bottle of champagne, a shopping bag filled with presents, and a pecan pie.

"You look beautiful," he said, as I took the pie from him.

"Thank you."

I had on a lacy red blouse with a camisole, and a short, black skirt. I'd also curled my hair, spent extra time on my makeup, and had splurged on a manicure.

"I'm kidnapping you later," he murmured, kissing me on the lips. "I need to see what's hiding under that sexy little skirt of yours."

"It's a surprise," I teased. I'd purchased a new red thong, along with a matching pushup bra at the mall, knowing he'd approve.

"Mm… I think I'm going to skip the pie and take you home early for a bite of yours," he said, sliding his free hand under my skirt.

"Stop," I giggled, pulling away.

He laughed.

"This looks really good. Did you make it?" I asked, looking down at it.

"Of course. I hope Vanda likes it," said Trevor as he followed me toward the kitchen. "You said it was her favorite."

"Oh, yeah. She goes absolutely *crazy* for pecan pie. You're going to win a lot of extra brownie points with this."

"I hope so. We're still telling her tonight, aren't we?"

"Yes," I said, my stomach twisting in knots at the thought of how she was going to react.

"Merry Christmas, Trevor," said Vanda, when we walked into

the kitchen. She was standing at the counter with Jim, drinking a glass of red wine.

"Merry Christmas," he replied. "You too, Jim."

"Thanks. Same to you," replied Jim, smiling.

"What do we have here?" asked Vanda, noticing the pie.

"Your favorite, Mom. Trevor made it."

Her eyes widened in surprise. "Pecan pie? You bake? Impressive."

He shrugged. "I bake a little."

"It looks wonderful," she said. "Thanks for bringing it. It looks wonderful."

"No problem."

"Can I take your jacket?" I asked, proud of his cooking abilities.

"Sure." Trevor took off his leather jacket and handed it to me. Underneath he wore a white knit sweater and a thick gold necklace that I didn't recognize.

"Where did you get the necklace?" I asked, staring at his neck.

He touched it. "My grandmother sent it. It's my Christmas gift."

"Oh, it's gorgeous," I replied. "She has good taste, too."

"I know. She's an amazing woman. Oh, by the way – what should I do with these?" he asked, nodding toward the paper bag. "I brought a couple of things."

I smiled. "I see that. I'll put them under our tree."

Vanda started asking him about his grandmother as I left the kitchen. After I returned, I noticed that she'd given him a beer and they were discussing food again. I could tell my mother was thrilled that he enjoyed cooking.

"I hope you like prime rib," she said, taking another drink of her wine.

"I love it," he replied.

"Good. I always make it on Christmas Eve. It's a holiday tradition, so you'd better get used to it."

"It smells great," he replied.

"Thank you. I used my mother's recipe, for the seasoning. She was an amazing cook."

"So are you," said Jim. "I think I've gained ten pounds since we started seeing each other."

"How long have you two been dating?" asked Trevor as he slipped his arm around my waist and pulled me in tightly.

"We started dating around the time that you did," said Vanda.

"Although... I'd been wanting to ask her out longer than that," added Jim, grabbing her hand and squeezing it.

"I don't blame you. In fact, I can see where Adriana gets her looks," said Trevor.

My mother blushed. "Nobody is as beautiful as my Adriana," she said.

"Thanks, Mom," I replied. "But, you're biased, obviously."

"You are beautiful," agreed Trevor, looking at me. "But, she definitely has your genes, Vanda. I only hope that our children take after your side of the family."

"I don't know what you're talking about," I said. "You're not so bad on the eyes."

He grinned. "It depends on the angle."

I laughed. "I've seen you from all angles and there is nothing ugly about you."

Vanda shook her head. "You two. With all of your good looks, I just hope you don't have girls. You'll need to guard them with your lives."

Trevor and I looked at each other. I nodded. Now was as good of time as any.

He stood up straighter. "It's funny that you should bring that up, because—"

"I'm having a baby," I blurted out.

My mother dropped her wine glass.

FORTY FOUR

FOUR

RAPTOR

"**F**UCK, I THOUGHT she was going to have a stroke when we told her about the baby," I said to Adriana as we drove to my house after dinner.

"She actually took it better than I thought she would."

"At least she let me stay," I joked. "It must have been the pie that saved me. Glad I made that."

"She loved the pie."

"I saw that. She's eating better now, isn't she?"

Adriana nodded.

"Did she ever talk to you about her headaches or what the doctor said about them?"

"We've both been so busy, with working and shopping, that I forgot to bring it up again. She seems like she's doing better, though."

"It if was important, I'm sure she'd tell you."

"I hope so. I'm definitely asking her about it when I get home."

"Who said I'm letting you go home?" I said and then gave a menacing laugh.

Adriana laughed. "You'll get sick of me in a couple of days."

"I would never get sick of you. Unless you try cooking for me again. I might have to kick you out, just so I can keep my house from burning to the ground."

The other day, Adriana had tried making breakfast and she'd started a towel on fire. I still wasn't sure how she'd managed to do it, but we'd decided that cooking wasn't her forte.

"Sorry about that," she said, smiling sheepishly. "I told you, I'm not good with that kind of stuff."

"It's okay. Your skills are in the bedroom. I'm more than happy to use mine in the kitchen."

"Your skills are in both rooms."

I grabbed her hand, the one with the engagement ring, and kissed it. "Glad you think so."

She spread her legs and moved my hand under her skirt. My cock sprang to attention as my fingers touched her panties.

"I bought a new thong," she said, sucking in her breath as I slid my finger under the silk.

"I hope you didn't pay too much because I'm about ready to rip it off of you, Kitten," I said, fingering her.

"Oh, my God," she moaned, opening her legs wider.

We were still miles from my house and I couldn't wait until then before I had her. Fortunately, we were near Horse's Auto Body shop and I had a spare key. I also knew his alarm code.

"Where are we going?" she asked as we took a detour.

"Somewhere close. Show me your pussy," I said.

She pulled the front of her panties to the side, showing me her sexy little landing strip.

"Touch yourself," I said, keeping one eye on the road and the other on her sex.

Adriana began rubbing her clit and I had to unbutton my jeans, I was so hard.

"Are we almost there?" she asked, reaching over to touch my cock.

"I think you are," I joked and then gasped as she squeezed the head of my penis. "Fuck, you'd better not do that or I'm going to crash the truck."

She removed her hand and went back to playing with herself, which didn't make things any easier for me. Fortunately, we made it to Horse's shop without dying.

"Why are we *here*?" she asked, looking out the window.

"Because I thought it would nice if I fucked you," I said, turning off the engine, "in a place that you've never been fucked before."

She giggled. "I think you've already hit every hole."

Smiling, I buttoned my jeans back up and we got out of the truck.

"Are you sure we won't get in any trouble?" she whispered, looking up at me as we walked toward the building.

"You're already in trouble," I said, putting my arm around her. "You feel me?"

She smiled wickedly and touched my zipper. "Oh, yeah... I feel you."

Grateful that Horse's shop was in a secluded area, I grabbed her by the elbow and guided her to the back door of the shop. I then opened the door and quickly turned off the alarm.

"This doesn't look like the best place for sex," said Adriana, not looking too sure.

"Don't worry, I know what I'm doing," I said, leading her through the garage, to Horse's office. He'd been boasting about a new leather sofa sleeper he'd had delivered to his office before the trip to Maui. A Christmas present to himself; one he hadn't properly broken in. I didn't think he'd be thrilled to learn that I was about to do the honors, but I was too horny to care at the moment.

"Whose office is this?"

"Horse's," I said, removing the sofa cushions. I pulled out the mattress and turned to her. "Ever do it on a sofa sleeper?"

"No."

"That's probably a good thing, but right now, it's all we have. Let's keep this to ourselves," I said, crawling onto the mattress. I turned around and grabbed her by the jacket, pulling her closer. "So, Horse doesn't find out and kill me."

Adriana giggled.

FORTY FIVE

ADRIANA

TREVOR PUSHED THE jacket off of my shoulders and then unbuttoned my red blouse. He pulled it off and then removed my camisole.

"New bra, too?" he asked in a husky voice. He was at eye level with my breasts and I could tell that he definitely approved.

I nodded.

He squeezed my breasts and then buried his face between them. Sighing in pleasure, I slid my hands behind his head as he rubbed his cheeks against my skin and then dragged his tongue into the valley between.

"You smell so good," he whispered.

"Thanks," I whispered back, running my fingers through his long hair.

Reaching around, he unclasped the back of my bra and pulled the cups away from my chest. Squeezing my breasts again, he bent his mouth over my nipple, circled it with his tongue, and then sucked the hard nub, making me moan in pleasure. He repeated it on the other breast, this time pulling my skirt up, too. Rolling my nipple between his teeth and tongue, he slid his hands over my ass and squeezed both cheeks, massaging them. As I moaned in approval, he slid one of his hands to my mound and pushed the front of my panty to the side. Touching my slicken labia, he groaned and slid one of his fingers into my hole.

"That feel good?" he whispered, adding a second finger.

"Yes," I said as he began fucking me with them. Moaning in pleasure, I grabbed his cock, which was at full mass and began stroking it, matching his movements. He sucked in his breath and allowed me to do it, but only briefly.

"You're no fun," I teased, when he made me stop.

"I'll show you fun."

Trevor pulled me with him onto the mattress and then turned over so that I was on my back. Placing my knees over his shoulders, he lowered his mouth to my clit and began to lick.

Gasping, I grabbed the top of his hair and whimpered in delight as his finger returned to my hole.

"Are we having fun now?"

"Yes," I gasped, as he added another finger.

His mouth returned to my clit and it was only a matter of time before I stiffened up, pulled his hair, and screamed out an orgasm.

Satisfied, Trevor got back onto his knees, wrapped my legs around his waist, and began fucking me, slowly.

"Faster," I demanded. Ever since he'd found out that I was pregnant, he'd been treating me like I was some kind of China doll and it was frustrating.

"You sure? I don't want to hurt you."

"You're not going to hurt me. Now, fuck me like you mean it or turn over so that I can take charge."

Before I knew what was happening, he flipped us over and I was sitting on top of him.

"So, you do want me to take charge?"

"Hell, yeah," he said, staring up at me. "Ride me, Kitten."

I began moving my hips, enjoying the way his face twisted with desire. He slid his hands up to my breasts and stared up at me.

"I love you so fucking much, Adriana."

"I love you, too," I replied, squeezing him with my pelvic muscles.

Sucking in his breath, he grabbed my waist and began thrusting himself, deeper and faster into me. Up and down I rode his cock, his face turning a deeper shade of red with each movement. After a few more thrusts, he rolled me off of him and got behind me.

"Yes," I moaned as he started fucking me, this time hitting my G-spot.

"Gonna come," growled Trevor, several thrusts later.

So was I.

The orgasm erupted inside of me and I could feel my vagina clench around his cock. Gasping, he stiffened up and joined me, his fingers holding my hips still as he emptied his seed into my womanhood.

"Good thing you're already pregnant," he said after catching his breath.

"Good thing," I replied, smiling.

Trevor kissed me and then started laughing.

"What's so funny?"

"There's cum all over this mattress now. Horse is going to kill me."

"Flip it over. He won't even notice," I said, getting off.

He smiled. "I knew there was a reason I fell in love with you."

"I hope there's more to it than that," I replied dryly.

"You're sexy. Great in bed…"

"And?"

He rubbed his chin. "You're an excellent cook?"

I gave him a dirty look.

"I'm just messing around. I love everything about you - your laugh, your sense of humor, your intelligence. But," he gave me a wicked grin, "I have to say, it doesn't hurt that you have nice tits."

"Wait until I start breast feeding. I heard they'll never be the same."

"That's okay, too," he said, touching them. "Because these breasts will be making our baby healthy and knowing that will only make them more beautiful."

I blinked back tears. "For someone who looks so bad-assed, you have a way with words."

"It's easy when someone like you inspires them."

Smiling, I leaned forward and kissed him on the lips.

FORTY SIX

ADRIANA

As we headed toward Trevor's house, he was unnaturally quiet.

"You okay?" I asked him.

"I'm just thinking about your mother. Do you think she's angry?"

"That I'm pregnant?"

He nodded.

"She's happy for us," I replied. "She told me so in the kitchen, when I helped her with the dishes."

"Did she? Good."

I reached over and grabbed his hand. "Thanks for being there tonight."

"It was my pleasure, Kitten. I had a great evening. I think your mom is actually starting to like me. "

"I think so, too. Good job on the scarf, by the way."

Trevor had given her a scarf for Christmas and she'd melted when she saw it. He'd given Jim a bottle of expensive brandy and me a beautiful tanzanite bracelet, one that he'd also purchased from Vanda.

"How did you know about the bracelet?" I asked.

"That you wanted it?"

"Yeah."

"Your mother, of course."

"I can't believe how much you've spent on me," I said. "And all I got you was a new wallet."

"It's not about the money. You know that."

"I know. Thank you... for everything."

"Of course. You deserve it and more. So, you think Vanda liked the scarf? I had a woman at Macy's help me pick it out."

"She loved it. You charmed the hell out of her tonight.

Although, the wine probably made you even more charming."

"You don't think I'm *naturally* charming?" he joked. "Wait, I have to fart."

"Don't you dare!" I cried, laughing. I rolled down the window, not smelling anything yet but not wanting to chance it.

"I'm joking," he said, also laughing. "Roll it back up. It's gotta be twenty degrees out there."

"You are such a shit," I said.

"You love me, though."

"Lord help me, I really do.

THREE MONTHS LATER

FORTY SEVEN

ADRIANA

"**D**O YOU WANT to know what you're having?" asked my Gynecologist.

Trevor and I both stared at the monitor in awe. I was having my first ultrasound and the image on the screen brought tears to my eyes. I looked at Trevor and noticed that he was pretty choked up himself. "Do we?"

"If you do, sure why not?" he said, holding my hand.

"I think we should," I said, excited. "What is it?"

"You're having a boy," she replied.

My heart filled with joy. I hadn't really cared what we were having before, but now that I knew for sure, I couldn't have been happier.

"A boy?" repeated Trevor, smiling proudly. "Really?"

She nodded. "See, there's the little boy part."

"Little? There won't be anything little about my son," said Trevor. "You're going to need a wider screen at the next ultrasound. Mark my words."

I snorted.

The doctor laughed. "I'll keep that in mind on our next scan."

We watched in awe as the baby moved around.

"This is so amazing," I said, touching the side of my stomach.

"So are you," said Trevor, bending over to kiss me on the lips. When he pulled away, I could see the tears in his eyes.

I smiled.

"Thank you. You gave me a son," he said, his voice breaking.

"You're going to be a wonderful father, Trevor."

Overcome with emotion, he looked away.

307

I let out a ragged breath, grateful for what we'd been given. A girl would have been loved just as much, but I knew deep down, he'd been hoping to have a boy, so that he could give his him the kind of life he'd dreamed of growing up. Now he could.

"Have you picked out any names yet?" asked the doctor.

"Samuel," said Trevor. He looked at me. "After your father."

I smiled.

FORTY EIGHT

ADRIANA

AMUEL JORDAN LARSEN was born on the fourth of August, after hours of unprogressive pushing. In the end, I needed an emergency C-section, in which Trevor stood by me the entire time, holding my hand.

"How big did they say he was?" I croaked, my voice hoarse after the ordeal.

"Eight pounds and two ounces," said Trevor.

"Sheesh. No wonder he wouldn't come out," I murmured, closing my eyes. I'd gotten a brief look at the baby before they'd whisked him away to clean him and check his vitals. From what I could tell, he was a beautiful baby, with black hair and a cute button nose.

"Told you my son was going to be big. You didn't believe me. Bet you'll never doubt me again."

"I doubt that," I teased, opening my eyes back up.

"Think you're funny, don't you?" he asked, squeezing my hand.

"Sometimes. You're an easy target."

"Mr. Larsen, would you like to give your son his first bath?" asked one of the nurses.

"Sure," he said, excited. "I'll be back, Adriana. You're okay?"

I nodded and closed my eyes, happy that it was finally over. It had been a stressful night and now all I wanted was to rest.

MY MOTHER AND Jim were waiting back in my hospital room when they wheeled me in.

"Do you want to hold your grandson?" asked Trevor, who was

carrying Samuel.

"Oh, my... yes," said Vanda, her eyes full of tears.

He handed her the baby and she smiled down at him. "So, this is Samuel? Aren't you a beautiful little boy..."

"Little? He was over eight pounds," boasted Trevor.

"I figured he'd be big after how big you were, these last couple of months, Adriana," said Vanda. "I almost thought there was a second baby hiding in your stomach."

"I know. I gained a lot of weight, but I was always hungry," I said, blushing. "I just couldn't help it."

"Don't worry, you did a fine job, Adriana," said Jim, standing next to her.

"She certainly did," said Trevor, grabbing my hand. "How are you feeling?"

"Good, but I'm sure it's because of the drugs," I replied. Something told me that after they wore off, I'd be hollering for more.

"Jim, give her the envelope," said my mother, as she rocked the baby in her arms.

Jim reached into his pocket and pulled it out.

"What's this?" I asked as he handed it to me.

"Open it," she said.

I opened it up and my jaw dropped. There were two airline tickets to Hawaii inside.

"That's so that you can elope or use them for your honeymoon," she said. "If you prefer."

We hadn't gotten married yet. I'd decided that I wanted to wait until after the baby was born.

"But we just had a baby. How can we leave him?" I protested.

"Don't worry, we'll watch Samuel," she said, smiling at Jim.

"Who's going to run the shop while you're watching Samuel?" I asked.

"I've hired a new manager," she said and smiled. "Tim."

"Why?" I asked, shocked.

"Remember when I fainted in the shop, last fall?" she said.

I nodded.

"My doctor told me that there was too much stress in my life and that I was working myself ragged. Now, I'm finally going to do something about it."

"What about your headaches?" I asked. "Was that stress related, too?"

"Yes," she replied and then looked embarrassed. "It also has to do with aging."

"Aging? Whatever. You're not that old," said Trevor.

"Thank you, I don't feel that old. Apparently, my body does, though," she said, chuckling.

"So, you're fine?" I asked, feeling a little ashamed that I hadn't even bothered to ask her about the headaches again.

"Fine enough to take Sammy here when you're on your honeymoon."

"Thanks, Vanda," said Trevor. He walked over and gave her a kiss on the cheek.

"You're welcome," she said, smiling.

"Yeah, thank you, Mom. For everything."

"You're welcome." She handed me Samuel and we both looked down into his face. "And thank you for giving me such a handsome grandson. You, too, Trevor. I can tell already that he's going to have your features."

"Thanks Vanda," he said.

She sat down next to me on the bed. "Being a parent doesn't always mean that you know what you're doing, Adriana. You learn as you go along. Even when your kids grow up, you sometimes make decisions that you regret later." She looked at Trevor. "Or assumptions about people when you shouldn't."

He smiled.

There was a knock on the door and Jim went to answer it.

"Hi, I'm Mavis," said a woman's voice. "I'm Trevor's mother."

Trevor swore under his breath.

"Come on in," called Vanda.

Mavis walked in. She was a little taller than my mother, but very thin and haggard looking.

I glanced up at Trevor. "Is this okay?" I whispered.

He didn't say anything but he looked angry.

Mavis walked into the room and gave me an apologetic look. "I'm sorry to barge in on you. I just wanted to see the baby. If that's okay?"

"Of course," I replied.

"How did you hear about this?" asked Trevor sternly.

"I called her," said my mother, smiling innocently.

"How did you get her number?" he asked, turning to look at Vanda.

"I spoke with your club president. Slammer," she answered. "Who should be arriving shortly, too. With Frannie."

"You know Frannie?" I asked, surprised.

She nodded. "Yes, she and I went to school together. I didn't realize it was the same woman whose wedding you attended in Maui. Anyway, they were in the shop last week and Slammer introduced himself. We got to talking and I found out that Slammer knew your mother, Trevor. He gave me Mavis's number. I hope you're not angry."

From the tense look on his face, I could tell he wasn't very happy about it. I grabbed his hand and squeezed it.

"Oh, he's beautiful," said Mavis, her eyes filling with tears. She took a tentative step toward the bed. "And, he looks just like you did when you were born, Trevor."

"You remember, huh?" he asked, a sneer on his face.

Mavis opened up her purse and took out an old photo. "Here, look," she said, ignoring his comment.

He took the picture and stared down at it.

"Let me see," I said, after a few seconds.

Trevor handed it to me, his expression unreadable.

I stared down at the photo and smiled. Our baby did look like his father. "You had dark hair when you were born, too. Just like Samuel."

He shrugged.

"Is that his name?" asked Mavis. "Samuel?"

"Yes," I said, kissing his forehead. "Samuel Jordan Larsen."

"He's beautiful," she said, staring at the baby longingly.

"Would you like to hold him?" asked Vanda.

Before she could answer, Trevor picked up Samuel and held him close to his chest.

"That's okay," said Mavis, her lips trembling. "I should probably go. I didn't want to interfere. I just wanted to see him."

"You wanted to see him? That's all?" asked Trevor, his eyes hard.

She nodded. "Yes. I'm sorry. I probably don't even deserve that much. Anyway, I'll leave you."

"You don't have to leave," I said, feeling sorry for her. "Really. You can stay."

"No," she said, blinking back tears. She looked back at Trevor. "You did well and I know you're going to be a wonderful father. Just don't make the same kinds of mistakes that we did."

"I won't," he said firmly.

She nodded and turned away.

"Wait," said Trevor, walking toward her.

Mavis turned around.

He held Samuel out. "I'm not going to make the same kinds of mistakes, which includes shutting out the people I love. Hold your grandson, Mavis."

She smiled, the tears streaming down her cheeks as he placed Samuel into her arms. "Oh, my... he's so beautiful. Hello, there, Samuel," she cooed, snuggling him against her chest.

Trevor turned around and our eyes locked. His face relaxed into a smile and I returned it.

I love you, I mouthed.

I love you, too, he mouthed back.

Just then, the door opened and a nurse walked in, carrying a gift box.

"Who's that from?" I asked, as she handed it to me.

"A man dropped it off,' she said. "It's for Samuel."

Trevor grabbed the envelope that was attached and opened it up. He read the card and his eyebrows shot up. "It's from Jordan."

I ripped the wrapping paper off of the box and we all stared at the little blue T-shirt. There was a picture of a gavel on the front and underneath it read "Don't Make Me Call My Uncle."

"Hey, at least he's acknowledging that he's an uncle," I said, smiling. "Maybe we can invite him over for the holidays this year? I bet he'd like that, you know?"

Trevor just laughed.

THE END

Made in the USA
Middletown, DE
19 June 2019